IMMORTAL

A Montague & Strong Detective Agency Novel

ORLANDO A. SANCHEZ

BITTEN PEACHES

ABOUT THE STORY

Killing an immortal is easy…once you know how.

Simon's past has returned, and she wants him dead.

Rejected by the Blood Hunters, Esti is looking to settle a debt against Simon and to do that, she's joined another group of vampire killers.

The Heretics of the Sanguinary Order.

The Sanguinary Order have given Esti control of an ancient creature—designed to negate magic—along with a stolen weapon created to kill immortals.

Joined by Dira--a successor to the Marked of Kali--Esti plans to destroy Simon Strong, filling his life with agony, before she ends him.

Now, together with Monty, Simon must find a way to stop a group of fanatical killers intent on his destruction, all without help from Kali, the goddess who created this mess in the first place.

Who wants to live forever?

"There can be only one."
-Juan Sanchez Villalobos Ramirez

DEDICATION

For the dreamers, who imagine living many lifetimes.

This is for you.

ONE

We sat parked in the center of Elk Street, a few blocks away from the Hellfire Club, staring at a series of barriers, which resembled enormous caltrops.

The orange runes on their surface pulsed in the dark.

"I don't remember those being there the last time we were in this neighborhood," I said, peering down the street. "Is that an art exhibition?"

"I don't think so," Monty said, looking behind us. "I'm noticing some runes behind the car. One second."

He stepped out of the Dark Goat and I did the same, opening the door for my ever-alert hellhound. Peaches bounded out and nudged past me throwing me off balance, and very likely saving my life.

I stumbled into the car as he muscled past me and the arrow meant for my chest, buried itself in my arm. I rolled to the drivers side of the Dark Goat and stayed crouched down, waiting for more arrows.

We took cover behind the Dark Goat.

"This is why we don't do housecalls," I said, as I gritted

my teeth against the pain throbbing in my arm. "Holy hell, this hurts."

"Whatever you do, do not pull it out," Monty said. "Let me look at it."

"Pull it out? No, of course not. I was thinking what color shirt I could wear with it, as an accessory. Why am I not pulling this thing out?" I asked as the pain radiated outward from my arm.

"There's a good chance that's a blood arrow," he said. "Didn't your vampire warn you about Esti being on the loose and looking for retribution?"

"She did, yes," I said with a short nod. "Next time, Erik comes to us asking for help, I' telling him, no. We are not the Montague and Strong delivery service."

"Do you intend to become a recluse?" he asked, ripping my shirt sleeve away from my arm. "You can't hide indoors indefinitely."

"Not indefinitely, just until my enemies get tired or die from boredom," I said, wincing when he pulled on my arm. "That shouldn't take too long."

"Not long at all, considering most of your enemies are on the longer-lived side," he said. "Shouldn't take more than a century or three."

"I'm not feeling the support here."

Peaches nudged his massive head against my side.

<What is it, boy?>

<I can pull the stick out of your arm. It's not very big. I can do it.>

<No, boy. That stick is dangerous and can explode. We're going to let Monty take care of this one.>

<His saliva can't heal you. My saliva can heal you. Do you want my saliva?>

<As amazing as that sounds, we're going to wait.>

<For what? The angry man is only looking at the stick. He should take it out then I can heal you with my saliva.>

<He's observing the best way to take it out.>
<He is looking too long. Does he want it to explode?>
<I really hope not. I'm kind of attached to my arm.>
<If you get hurt, I will heal you.>
<Let's hope it doesn't come to that, slide over a bit and let him get a closer look.>

My hellhound shifted over to the side giving Monty more access to the arrow.

"This does not look good," he said, slowly lifting my arm and examining the arrow. "At least it missed all the important bits. That is one *nasty*-looking arrow however. I need to take a closer look at the runes on the shaft."

"Is that your official observation, doctor?" I asked as a wave of arrows rained down on the Dark Goat. "Looks like we have their attention now."

Monty looked behind the Dark Goat at the runes that initially drew his attention and shook his head.

"Clever," he said. "Those runes are keyed to your particular energy signature. If we had attempted to reverse the vehicle, they would have…" —he traced a trail of runes with his gaze and finger, pointing at the adjacent building— "brought that building down on us. It may not have destroyed the car, but it could have trapped us inside."

"Someone did their homework," I said, seeing the symbols etched into the street and following his hand to where the symbols ended around the base of the building next to us. "That is some evil runic BS."

"The runes are not evil—"

"Don't start," I snapped. "It would have brought the building down on us in an attempt to squash us. I call that evil. It could have killed who knows how many innocent bystanders—that is evil."

"I'm not necessarily disagreeing with you," he said, gazing around us. "The runes themselves are not evil, but the way they are implemented certainly speaks to someone who wishes you ill will."

"Ill will?" I said, pointing at the arrow. "We're calling this ill will?"

"What would you call it?

"Where I come from, burying an arrow in someone is a good way to get killed. This was a trap and I stepped right into it. If Peaches hadn't shoved me to one side, this arrow would be in my chest or neck," I said. "I call this attempted murder."

"I'm inclined to agree with you," he said, gazing up to the roofs of the buildings around us. "Whoever shot you didn't count on your sudden movement."

"Hard to adjust for irregular movements with an arrow," I said, glancing at the arrow. "But whoever did it, they're good. Anyone but the best shot would've missed me entirely. This archer adapted and modified the shot in a split-second."

"They picked the right street, but I have to assume, if they were thorough, that all of the streets leading away from the Hellfire Club were similarly trapped."

"It's a good trap especially if what you said about being keyed to my energy signature is true," I said. "It's the ultimate passive destructive system. Wait until I'm in the area and activate the runes to go off when I walk or drive by. They knew we were driving, though, or else why use those barriers at the other end of the street."

"Indeed," he said. "It's too elaborate to be spur of the moment."

"Where is everyone?" I looked around realizing there wasn't anyone out here. "Aversion runes?"

"Good question," he said. "It would seem they somehow managed to empty this and the adjoining streets. That takes planning."

The street around us was deserted, which normally

wouldn't have caught my attention, except we lived in the city that didn't sleep. Deserted streets weren't a thing, even in the middle of the night.

"Don't you think it's a little weird that the streets are empty?" I asked, glancing to the left and right. "When are the streets ever empty like this?"

"When an ambush that has been put in place to attack you and it has been sprung, it seems," Monty said. "I'm not noticing any aversion runes. They must have used more conventional means. Perhaps more of those barriers to prevent pedestrian and vehicular traffic. What seems more relevant, however, is how did they know you would be coming down this *particular* street?"

"That's a great question," I said with a wince. "Maybe we can ask our friendly archer how she pulled that little trick off?"

"Are you certain it's a she?"

"I haven't pissed off any male archers recently, and the only group I know of that enjoys going medieval with arrows on targets are the Blood Hunters, and they're all female."

"Good deduction," he said with a nod. "I do believe you are correct."

I shifted to one side as my arm screamed at me.

"Be still," Monty said as he leaned in to get a better look at the arrow. "This is going to be tricky."

"Tricky?" I said. "I have an arrow buried in my arm...it looks real similar to an *explosive* arrow, Monty. Remember those?"

"I'm aware of what kind of arrow," he said, his voice tight. "It would seem the Blood Hunters have decided to express their displeasure with you...again."

"Thinking about it, I doubt this is them," I said with another wince as Monty lightly touched the arrow in my arm.

"This is most likely Esti and her psychotic crew of extreme hunters, what was it again—the Sanitary Order?"

"Sanguinary," Monty corrected. "And I believe they are called Heretics."

"Yes, them," I said. "Any group insane enough to take Esti as one of their members has to be deranged."

"If you would stop moving, it would make reading these runes easier. That way I can deactivate them."

"Oh, I'm *sorry*," I said. "My moving is making it difficult for *you* to read the runes. You mean the runes, on the *arrow*, which is *buried* in my arm?"

"Stop moving," he warned. "I realize this is uncomfortable, but I have to get an idea of what I'm dealing with here before I attempt to remove it, without removing your arm."

"I like that last part," I said. "The 'not removing my arm' part."

"Then keep *still*," he said, holding the shaft of the arrow steady as I shifted again. "This appears to be a variant of the blood arrows that the Blood Hunters use."

"It's not like I *want* to move," I said, gritting my teeth. "I have a severe allergy to arrows puncturing any part of my body. Especially when those arrows can explode and remove said body part. You think Esti is trying to tell me something?"

"It is possible she may be trying to convey her desire for vengeance for what you did," he answered. "However, I highly doubt Esti fired this arrow. Considering her animosity toward you, I feel she would have aimed for somewhere more...final."

"Final?"

"Your eye, or neck, or more likely your heart," he answered in his clinical Spock voice. "I do have to wonder how she would manage it with one arm. Most likely she'd have used some modified weapon or some kind of crossbow to be effective. It does bear some investigating."

"I'm glad you find all this so fascinating, Spock," I said.

"You know what I wonder? I wonder how much longer do you need to 'read' the arrow before we get started on the *removal* part of the process?"

"No need to get testy," he said. "I was merely stating that the odds of Esti being the perpetrator of this attack are high. You can't deny she bears you ill will—you did relieve her of an arm."

"She was trying to kill Chi," I said. "If you ask me, she got off easy. I only took her arm, I should have removed her head. She walked away with her life."

"Some people tend to hold grudges about those sorts of things."

"Which? Esti trying to kill Chi, or me removing her arm?"

"Both."

"True," I said with a brief nod as another set of arrows sliced silently through the night, bouncing off the far side of the Dark Goat. "I have their general direction, but we don't know—"

"If those are the only hunters in the area," Monty finished, his attention on the arrow. "Let's focus on the priority. Internal then external. We extricate the arrow first, then address the enemies trying to explosively end your existence."

"Was that mage humor?"

"Merely stating the obvious," he deadpanned. "It's only logical we address our attackers *after* the arrow is removed."

"That would be excellent," I said as sweat formed on my brow. "Without exploding my arm to bits."

"Without exploding your arm to bits," he repeated. "Then we deal with whomever is firing arrows at you. I have to say, you have a singular way of making friends that leaves much to be desired."

I glared at him.

"First, not my friends. Second, can *you* really talk about

making friends?" I asked. "Your track record is far from excellent."

"Par for the course," he said, waving my words away. "I'm a battle mage, we don't make friends. They're either enemies or enemies in waiting."

Peaches whined next to me.

The whine quickly shifted to a growl when he sniffed the air.

<Whoever hurt you is close. I can chew on them and hurt them back.>

<No, boy. They may have something that can hurt you. Stay close until we figure out what's going on.>

"What is troubling your creature?"

"You mean besides the arrow in my arm?"

"Yes," he said with a sigh, "besides the arrow. I have seen you take more damage than this arrow. Aren't you being a bit dramatic?"

"It's not the damage, it's the potential explosion," I said. "He says he can pinpoint where the archer is and can go visit them with a friendly mauling."

"I'd advise against it," he said with another gesture that formed a golden orb near my arm. "They may try to apprehend him, or worse."

"I told him to stay close until we knew more about what was going on," I said. "Why would they attack us now? When I say now, I mean in the general sense. If it's Esti, she has to know this won't bring her arm back."

"It could be a status thing," he said. "She lost her position after her failed attempt on your vampire. It's possible she's trying to re-establish her lost position."

"I seriously doubt the Blood Hunters would accept her back," I said. "Isn't that why she joined the Sandwich Order?"

He stared at me for a good three seconds before shaking his head.

"You're doing that deliberately, aren't you?"

"Doing what?" I said, keeping my expression innocent. "I was just wondering why the Blood Hunters would even consider taking her back—she was horrible for their reputation."

"Good question," he said, gently nudging the orb closer to the arrow shaft. "Aside from the whole arm removal thing, didn't you say your vampire mentioned an imminent attack?"

"She did," I said, eyeing the orb warily. "What is that orb supposed to do?"

"It's going to excise the head of the arrow," he said, focused on the arrowhead as he lifted my arm gently. "That should allow for removal and destruction of the rest of the blood arrow."

"Is there any reason we can't do this inside the Dark Goat?"

"Normally, I would say no, but some of these runes look reactive."

"Which means?"

"The runes Cecil placed inside the Dark Goat could trigger a detonation," he said. "As I said, this seems to be a more lethal variant of the blood arrows used in the past."

"Wonderful, they upgraded their arrows just for me. I feel extra special now," I said. "Is that the reason for the orb, and you not disintegrating this thing with some finger-wiggles?"

"Astute," he said. "The same precautions apply. If I try to disintegrate or directly affect the arrow with a cast, it may react and explode, taking your arm with it."

"I'll have to thank Esti personally for this detonative demonstration of her deranged and demented desire for my death."

Monty nodded in appreciation.

"Well done," he said. "Full marks on the alliteration."

"Glad I could impress," I said. "Do you know what would be really impressive?"

"I have an idea. Perhaps if you stopped distracting me?"

I remained silent and thought about the warning Chi had given me recently.

Esti was coming for me, and she didn't care who or what got in her way. The fact that she was willing to drop a building on me was a clear indicator of how serious she was.

More to the point, she was unhinged.

I recalled she was psychotic enough to disregard Archmage Julien's warning about not bringing weapons into his home.

Not only did she bring weapons, but she also proceeded to attack us with them. The fact that now some fringe Order accepted her, when even the Blood Hunters had kicked her out, was bad news.

I looked down at the arrow buried in my arm.

Monty was right. This arrow, though similar, wasn't the same.

If possible, this was an even nastier piece of work than the last time I played target for the Blood Hunters and had one of these exploding arrows buried in my leg.

The fletching on this one was made of red and black feathers. The metal shaft was covered in softly pulsing orange runes which, despite the fact that I couldn't decipher them, looked dangerous and volatile. The head of the arrow appeared to be made of onyx.

"These blood arrows do seem to be an upgrade from the last time I wore one as an accessory," I said. "Do you know how much of an upgrade?"

"These are worse, if I'm reading these runes correctly."

"Worse, of course, why would I expect anything else?" I said. "What was I thinking? Worse how, exactly?"

"I ask myself that same question regarding your thought

processes on a daily basis," he said. "Like the previous blood arrows we're familiar with, the runes on this arrow mix with the blood of the victim."

"But?" I asked. "I'm sensing a major *but* in that description."

"Well, I don't want to alarm you—"

I stared at him and gave him a flinty Clint Glint. At the very least a two, if not a two point five, on the glare-o-meter.

"Alarm me? Monty," I said, keeping my voice as calm as possible, "I have a group of unstable, angry women, led by a deranged psychotrix bent on vengeance—doing their best to make me impersonate a porcupine. I am *way* past alarmed and fast approaching terrified. I'm just remaining calm so *you* don't lose it."

"How considerate of you," he said. "Thinking of my well-being that way is magnanimous."

"I try," I said, "now stop stalling and spill it. "How bad is it?"

"Very well, the previous blood arrows we encountered would detonate when exposed to air, catalyzing the blood and creating a substantial explosion. Do you recall?"

"I recall," I said. "How is this one worse?"

"See the pulsing orange runes along the shaft?"

"I have."

"Have you noticed that they are slowly becoming dim, starting at the fletching and descending it appears, to the arrowhead?"

The realization dawned on me.

I was looking at a countdown.

"It's a timer, isn't it?"

He nodded solemnly.

"Seems to be, yes," he said. "It appears we are limited on time."

As he said that, the orange runes still softly glowing around the fletching, became dim and stopped pulsing.

"Monty?" I said, with possibly the slightest bit of hysteria in my voice. "Have I mentioned that I really want this arrow out of my arm? Before the runes go dim and blow me up?"

"The placement of this blood arrow is highly suspect," he said, still examining the runes. "Why not shoot you in the chest or the neck? Even if you had shifted suddenly, a second shot could have been in placed almost immediately. While I agree Esti may be behind this attack, why not incapacitate you immediately, then remove your arm?"

"Maybe she hasn't put as much thought into this as you have?" I said. "Can we do less with the theorizing, and more with the deactivating and removing?"

"If this works, then we can get this arrow out of your arm."

"What do you mean, '*if this works*'?" I said. "You're not sure?"

"Well, the theory is sound, but I don't make a practice of defusing or deactivating detonative arrows as a regular activity."

"Did you just use my word?" I asked. "And what do you mean, '*the theory is sound*'? You actually don't know?"

"No, not really," he said, pointing at the shaft. "We're running out of time. If we delay further, this conversation is bound to reach an explosive conclusion."

"Pass on going out with a bang," I said. "Do what you need to do and I hope you're right."

"As do I," he said, not filling me with any kind of confidence. "At least we'll know immediately if your new nickname will be Lefty."

"Wonderful, more mage humor."

"If this orb sets off the reactive runes, the effect will be instantaneous."

"There's no way to slow the countdown?"

"None that I can see, but I'm no expert on these things."

"Have I told you that your attempts at humor and distraction truly suck?"

"Repeatedly," he said. "Are *you* done stalling?"

"I'm not stalling," I said. "I'm just delaying a bit to wrap my head around losing an arm, if this method of yours doesn't work."

He raised an eyebrow at me.

"Fine," I said with a sigh and took hold of my hellhound's scruff as he rumbled assurance at me. "Do it."

"Understood," he said, becoming serious. "Brace yourself."

He gestured and formed a series of tight, golden lattices around my arm. They layered over each other, and I realized they were designed to contain the explosion if the orb set off the arrow.

He touched the orb and it slowly expanded, enveloping my arm and the arrowhead. I winced in anticipation of an explosion, but nothing happened.

"So far, so good," he said. I noticed sweat had formed on his brow too. "Next phase is the excision. The orb will collapse around the arrowhead and I will remove the rest of the arrow in one move. As much as possible, stay behind the Dark Goat."

I nodded.

The time for words had passed.

TWO

Monty took hold of the arrow shaft and I grunted in pain.

The orb, which had been about the size of a grapefruit, had begun to shrink around the arrowhead and part of the shaft.

It began to glow, bright enough that I had to look away.

"This is going to happen in two phases," Monty said, keeping his grip on the arrow shaft. "The orb is going to cut and contain the arrowhead, which appears to be the primary catalyst for the detonation. At the same time, I'm going to pull the shaft out of your arm."

"You're telling me this because…?"

"Because there's a chance the arrow could explode the moment the arrowhead is cut," he said. "If I sense that is the case—that an explosion is imminent—I will be forced to take alternative actions."

"Like?"

"It's complicated," he said. "Do you really want me to get into the details now?"

"Yes."

He looked at the arrow and the rapidly shrinking orb and motioned with his head.

"Really?" he continued. "Now?"

"If I can lose an arm, then yes," I said. "Give me the *Reader's Digest* version."

"For your information, no one reads those anymore."

"Then make it the *CliffsNotes* version," I insisted. "I want to know what you plan on doing in the next ten seconds."

He stared at me for a second and shook his head.

"It's called a tethered shunt," he said. "The best way to think of it is—imagine a yoyo and string."

"I'm the string?"

"No, you're the yoyo," he explained. "If I sense the arrow is going to explode, I activate the shunt."

"That pushes me away?"

"Far enough to avoid losing your arm, I hope."

"What happens to the arrow?" I asked, curious because at no point did he mention disintegrating the arrow. From his description of this tethered shunt, it sounded like—

"Yes, in case you were wondering, I will be holding onto the arrow shaft."

"As it explodes?" I said. "No, Monty. I can't let you do this."

"I don't recall asking your permission," he said, his voice hard. "You do realize you don't need to be conscious for this to occur? I could always incapacitate you for this part. Probably be easier if I did; it would certainly be quieter."

"You wouldn't."

"You like your arm...attached, that is?"

"Yes, it's my preferred choice when it comes to my limbs."

"Then the tethered shunt is a precaution I need to have in place. Think of it as a contingency plan for an unexpected explosion. Now, if you could stop talking and let me focus. I have no intention of exploding myself over Esti's hatred for you."

"Good, I was concerned there for a second."

"Noted," he said, focusing on the arrowhead and the shaft. "The orb will increase in temperature shortly, then we only have a few seconds before it cuts through the shaft."

The orb had shrunk down to surround the arrowhead and began giving off an incredible amount of heat.

"It's getting hot," I said, slowly moving my arm away from my body. "Okay, it's past getting hot and burning me now."

"Good, brace yourself, we are entering uncharted territory," he said. "I daresay we are boldly entering a phase where no one has gone before."

I stared at him.

"You didn't just—"

I never finished the sentence.

Several things happened all at once.

The orb sliced through the shaft. At the same time, Monty gripped the rest of it, as all of the runes went dim, and pulled it out of my arm. I saw the expression on his face—it was a mix of: *bollocks* and *bloody hell*. He gestured and I felt myself slide away from him, Peaches and the arrow.

Along with the safety provided by the cover of the Dark Goat.

He gestured again and created a shield that partially covered me, deflecting several arrows from my body. Then he stepped away from the Dark Goat and drew fire.

The arrows never reached him. He unleashed a small whirlwind of golden energy near where he stood. The whirlwind pushed and deflected arrows away from him as he whispered something over the arrow shaft.

He reached back and threw the arrow shaft in the direction the arrows were coming from, just as I felt myself come to a sudden stop and reverse direction.

Several arrows punctured the asphalt where I was a moment earlier. I tumbled behind the Dark Goat as the night briefly became day and the arrow exploded in the sky. The explosion washed over our location, rocking us and the Dark Goat.

The force of the blast shoved us back, but we quickly recovered, taking cover. I felt the flush of heat in my body, as my curse kicked in and started healing me.

"Judging from the force of that blast, I'd say that arrow is a considerable upgrade," he said. "It would have removed more than your arm."

"Note to self: do not get punctured by these new and improved blood arrows."

"A good policy," he said. "One I strongly suggest you adhere to."

"Can we get the Dark Goat out?" I asked, looking down the street at the metal debris blocking the street. "What exactly are those things?"

"If memory serves, I believe those are smaller versions of Czech Hedgehogs," he said, peering over at the obstacles. "These come equipped with runic components. I have to say that the Sanguinary Order seems better equipped than the Blood Hunters."

"Of course they do. Can you remove these barriers?"

"Not without exposing myself," he said, looking down at the other end of the street. "I believe that's why they were deployed, to stall us until *that* arrived."

"What are you...holy hell, what is that?" I said, looking down the street. I didn't get a good look, but the energy signature that was approaching us was off-the-charts in the you-should-be-scared-witless category. "Monty, what is coming our way?"

"It can't be..." he said, staring down the street. "I haven't

—not since the war—I never thought I would sense one of those in my life again."

Peaches whined and growled and stepped closer to me.

"Goodbye, Strong," a voice called out into the night. "I'm going to enjoy watching you die."

It sounded like a deranged Esti, which meant it was her usual voice.

"That you, Esti?" I called out. "Your arrow failed by the way. I still have all my parts attached. I've been meaning to ask you: What is the sound of one hand clapping?"

Another barrage of arrows was my answer, forcing me to take cover behind the Dark Goat again.

"Having you explode would have been a nice consolation," she called back. "But that wasn't the point of the arrow. I needed you in one place long enough for my creature to get here. I think you'll like him. Some of the sorcerers in the Order created it long ago specifically to deal with hard to kill targets and I recently released it."

Her words gave me pause.

"Monty? Anything in that wikibrain of yours about creatures created to deal with hard to kill targets?"

"Plenty," he said, focused on the street behind us. "I think we need to get into the car. Right now."

A roar filled the night, shattering some of the windows and rattling the others. The footsteps of whatever was coming down the street sounded like an angry, deeper-toned, pile driver.

Each step sent a small tremor our way.

The tremors felt like advanced physical promises of the impending pain and death heading our way. Monty's idea of getting into the car sounded excellent. I grabbed the rear door handle and pulled it open.

"Inside, boy."

My hellhound refused to budge.

Peaches growled, standing his ground. Above us, I heard Esti laugh into the night.

"Time to die, Strong."

<The bad monster is coming. I can bite it.>

<No, boy. I think this is one fight where we tactically place as much distance between us and the monster as possible.>

<I am a hellhound. I do not run from danger. You are my bondmate. You do not run from danger. We do not run from danger, we run into danger.>

<Not tonight, we don't.>

<Why not? You are stronger now.>

<Not that strong.>

<You are not scared, I know this. Why do we retreat?>

<Simple. I am not a hellhound, and this danger looks like it could stomp all of us. That means we retreat until we figure out what it is and how to stop it. I promise you, I'll let you bite it, blast it, and chomp it later, just not tonight.>

An enormous shadow fell over the south end of the street.

"Bloody hell," Monty said, pulling his door open. "Simon, get your creature into the car, now!"

I shoved Peaches into the Dark Goat.

He had grown in recent months.

This was what happened when you fed an ever-hungry hellhound a steady diet of choice meat. He didn't become fat; it was closer to his body transforming into a smaller version of his dad. I was currently the bondmate to a mini-Cerberus.

Peaches had grown to the point that I'd need a small crane to lift him. My 'shove' was really more of a suggested nudge. If he didn't want to move, there was no way I could move him.

Thankfully, he jumped into the Dark Goat.

He was right though, I wasn't scared, not really. After everything Monty and I had faced—fear, real fear, took a while to kick into gear in my brain.

I wouldn't call it being fearless, more like being immune to the voice of reason and caution. It was that same voice that was currently trying to get my attention by tapping on my brain somewhere near the defective fight or flight region, and trying to activate the flight section with a sledgehammer.

It pointed out that I had missed the near-hysteria and fear in Monty's voice.

I hadn't missed it, but I was angry.

I didn't like being anyone's target, and Esti, who should've been a memory, was out roaming the streets of my city and targeting me and mine.

Well, mostly me.

"Why don't you come down and face me," I said as Monty began gesturing and giving me the *this is not the time or place to get into it with the psychotic Blood Hunter, death is coming* look. I ignored him. "I'm right here. You still have one arm, bring a blade and face me."

"If you manage to survive my pet, and I truly do hope you survive, I will find you," she said with a small laugh. "You can't hide from me, Simon. I can *always* find you."

Something about the way she said those last words sent chills down my spine. The black and red energy rushing out from Monty's hands immediately grabbed my attention.

"Monty?" I said in concern as I whirled in his direction. "What the hell are you doing?"

"Keeping us alive!" he hissed. "Get in the bloody car, now!"

The black and red energy raced over the street and headed toward the creature. A few moments later, it rose off the street, blocking it, and created a black and red energy lattice, which crackled with power.

I jumped into the car and crawled over to the driver's side.

THREE

"We need to go, now!" he said. "Before it gets too close and it's over."

"I'm all for the evacuation plan," I said, looking behind us. "That thing—I'm guessing you know what it is—it's blocking the street behind us. And whatever you just did with your wiggle-fingers is adding another layer of impossibility. Is that a wall of black and red energy?"

"Not *that* way, Simon," he said, pointing forward. "We have to go through the barriers."

"The barriers?" I said. "The ones designed to stop tanks? In case you haven't noticed, the Dark Goat is not even a tank."

He glanced back for half-a-second and shook his head, murmuring something under his breath I didn't quite catch.

"It can't be helped," he said. "We cannot go back that way. Not if we want to survive this night. Bloody hell, I never thought I'd see one of those again. I thought summoning them had been rendered impossible."

"Monty? You're making me nervous," I said. "And considering everything we've seen and dealt with, for you to be concerned is concerning."

He turned to face me, a somber expression on his face.

"Oh, I'm making you *nervous,* am I? Good. That creature back there, which is currently headed our way to end our existence, is a Demogre," he said, his voice hard. "They were a scourge during the war, slaughtering mages by the dozens. They are the stuff of nightmares."

He said the name of the creature as if I understood what he meant and would tremble appropriately. The entire basis for my concern was in the tone of his voice.

I've seen Monty in several moods, most of them variations of angry or cranky or some combination of both. Right now, there was a serious undercurrent of heightened concern, which for us non-mages would usually be expressed as losing our minds from fear.

I still didn't know what he was talking about.

"It's a what? A demi ogre?" I asked, starting the Dark Goat. "Does that mean it's smaller than regular ogres?"

The roar of the engine filled the street.

There was no basking when death was coming for us.

"Demogre not demi-ogre, one word," he said, gesturing again. "It's a demonic ogre with all the horror that entails. It's intelligent and possesses the ability to cast at near Archmage level."

"It can cast?" I said, shocked. "Who is insane enough to combine a demon and an ogre? Know what, don't bother answering that. Did you say Archmage level?"

"*Near* Archmage," he corrected as if that was any better. "It gets worse."

"How can it possibly get any worse?"

"I thought you knew this by now, it can always get worse."

"It can always get worse," I said with a nod. "That basically explains my life. How does it get worse?"

"Demogres are banned weapons of war," he continued, glancing back every few seconds. "They were created to deal with mages or any beings who wielded magic. A sort of last resort against mages."

"Why does this sound so much worse than near-Archmage levels of casting?"

"Because it is, Demogres inherently exude a null field around their bodies," he said. "It has an area-of-effect of a hundred feet, rendering all magic and energy manipulation around it impossible. It was created to be a mage-killer."

I gave this description some thought.

"You're saying it's a walking neutral zone?"

He nodded, still focused on his gestures.

"My casts would be rendered null and ineffective," he said. "We would have to employ our seraph weapons, which are the only practical defense against creatures of this type."

"In case you haven't noticed, our weapons are designed for close-quarter combat," I said. "How close do we want to be to this thing?"

"If it's currently down the street, the ideal distance would be Canada."

I shot him a glance to see if he'd had some kind of mental episode and just attempted a joke. Then I came back to my senses and remembered that Monty doesn't make jokes.

He was serious.

Then, another realization hit me.

My curse was based on what Kali had done to me. On some level, I had to figure magic or energy manipulation was involved. If this Demogre neutralized all magic in an area-of-effect around it, would it remove my curse, rendering me mortal?

"Holy hell," I said in a half whisper. "Do you think my curse would be affected? Would it remove it?"

"I don't know," he said. "You were cursed by a goddess. I

wouldn't exactly consider Kali a mage, and if she were, she would surpass Archmage level by several orders of magnitude. However there is always the chance. Would you like to remain here and find out? I'm certain the Demogre would be willing to accommodate your curiosity as it rips your arms off."

"Not really, no," I said. "Here's an idea." I pointed out the windshield. "We go through those barriers."

"A wonderful idea," he said, strapping in. "Why didn't I think of it?"

I shook my head as I patted the Dark Goat's dash.

"This is either going to demonstrate that Cecil deserves to be called a grandmaster of his craft, or it's going to be one of our shortest attempts at escape, as we go from eighty to zero in less than one second."

"I'll place my faith and trust in Cecil's craftsmanship over our ability to face and destroy that Demogre tonight," he said. "We are not ready to take that thing on."

"*Tonight?*" I asked incredulously. "How about never?"

"I'm afraid that's not an option, especially if Esti is controlling it."

"Do you know how to fight it?" I asked, glancing back at the lattice of black and red energy blocking the street behind us. "You know how to beat it?"

"I'll tell you all about it, once we get past those barriers," he said, his voice tight as he glanced behind us again. "Drive, Simon, that lattice won't stop it for long."

Another roar filled the night, this one louder than the roar of the Dark Goat's engine. In my peripheral vision, I saw Monty gesture again, as the runes inside the Dark Goat bloomed to life, first turning orange, followed by red, and then a deep violet.

"What was that?"

"*That* was the signal to drive," he said, still gesturing. "Unless you want to test your immortality on this street."

I floored the gas pedal.

I sped toward at the Hedgehog barriers, determined to either obliterate the Dark Goat or ram through them. I knew no ordinary vehicle was going to get through, but the Dark Goat was no ordinary vehicle.

I tightened my grip on the wheel, and Monty continued to gesture while adding some words under his breath I didn't quite catch.

We raced down the street, and the world compressed in my vision to the series of Hedgehogs blocking our way.

I said a silent prayer to Wolverine, my patron saint of badassery. If we ever needed a moment of invincibility, it was now. I stomped on the gas pedal, and strangled the steering wheel with both hands, my knuckles turning white, and headed for the center Hedgehog.

The runes inside the Dark Goat grew a deeper violet with a tinge of red and orange as we collided with the Hedgehog. For a brief moment, the Hedgehog held, and I thought we were going to be stuck while the Demogre caught up to us and crushed the Dark Goat with us inside of it.

A few seconds after the initial collision, the runes on the barrier exploded with orange light which grew brighter by the second. I kept pressing the accelerator while Monty gestured.

Cecil was truly a grandmaster of his craft.

"Whatever you do, do *not* take your foot off that pedal," Monty said, his voice strained. "We just need a little longer."

Five seconds later—which felt like a lifetime—the runes on the barrier winked out. The Hedgehog, which was made of a bunch of I-beams welded together at right angles, flew apart into several pieces.

This left a hole in the barrier wall for the Dark Goat.

A hole I intended to exploit.

The Dark Goat shot forward as if we had been launched like a rocket. As we raced down the street, a barrage of arrows peppered the Dark Goat. I laughed, as we picked up speed. If the Dark Goat could muscle through that Hedgehog, would a bunch of exploding blood arrows do?

Not much to us, but then again I quickly realized they weren't aiming at us. The first indication was the large explosion, which caused me to swerve away from the crater that formed directly in front of us.

"Get us off this street," Monty said as he whispered something under his breath and pointed ahead of us. "This cast won't last long."

A golden honeycomb pattern formed in front of the Dark Goat, covering the street as we raced away from the Demogre and Esti. I reached the end of Elk Street, pulled a hard right onto Reade Street for a short block, and then swerved onto Centre Street, heading uptown and away from death.

FOUR

"How did Esti get ahold of a Demogre?" I said, trying to keep calm as I heard the roar behind us. "You said they were banned, right?"

"Banned doesn't mean extinct," Monty answered matter-of-factly. "The question is not how she got ahold of one, but rather, how is she controlling it? Demogres operate on a power structure. They only respect superior power. I don't recall Esti wielding that level of power."

We raced up Centre Street until I was sure the Demogre wasn't chasing us anymore.

"You can reduce the velocity to not-escaping-a-certain-death," Monty said, glancing behind us. "The only saving grace of confronting those creatures is that they're slow. Well, slow but inevitable."

"Meaning?"

"During the war, they were known as Death Ogres," Monty said. "If one of them locked onto a target, it could follow that signature anywhere."

"Anywhere?"

"If it had keyed onto you, there would be nowhere for us

to run that it couldn't follow," he said. "We would have to venture off-plane, and even then, it would probably still be able to follow us."

"Something she said stuck with me," I said as we headed uptown. "She said: 'You can't hide from me, Simon. I can always find you.'"

"I recall," he said, pensive. "We need to have you scanned."

"Scanned?"

"She's not a mage," he said. "She shouldn't possess the ability to track you wherever you are, yet—"

"She found me on that street," I said. "How?"

"An excellent question. Look out!" he yelled as a young woman appeared in the middle of the street, directly in front of the Dark Goat. "No!"

It was too late to swerve away, she was too close, and I had no time to react. I instinctively assessed the situation and realized it was a no-win scenario.

There was no time and not enough street to avoid her.

Still, I tried.

I yanked the wheel hard to the left.

The Dark Goat responded, but we were going too fast. The momentum kept carrying us forward into a drift. We were going to hit her broadside. Four thousand pounds of Dark Goat was going to absolutely crush this woman where she stood.

Shit, she's going to die.

We were out of options and time.

I did the only thing I could think of in the moment and really hoped it would work.

I pressed my mark.

The symbol on my hand exploded with white light, shifting the runes inside the Dark Goat from violet to bright white and nearly blinding me in the process.

That's never happened before.

The Dark Goat didn't stop.

In fact, nothing stopped as we slid right into…and through the woman. We slid for several more feet before it felt as if a giant hand had reached out and brought us to a sudden stop.

I reluctantly looked out the driver's side window, expecting a gore fest in the middle of Centre Street when I noticed the woman still standing there.

She was smiling at me.

"Impossible," I whispered to myself. "How did I miss—?"

"You didn't miss," she said. "You never hit me."

She beckoned me forward with a finger as the driver's side door was flung open. I hesitated exiting the car.

I was fairly certain she wasn't human.

No one with normal reflexes could have avoided the Dark Goat. There wasn't enough time. Which meant I was facing some kind of *entity*.

My track record with entities of power has been horrible so far. If they weren't trying to kill me, they were making unrealistic demands of me.

If it wasn't either of those, I was was being given titles, which I think they thought was something I appreciated.

I didn't.

All of these titles meant more responsibility on my already overburdened life.

It was difficult enough being immortal.

When you added being the *Aspis*, the Marked of Kali, a bondmate to a hellhound, the bearer of a necrotic seraph blade—which seemed to be on the verge of becoming sentient, and that the sentience belonged to a bloodthirsty goddess who was very likely the first vampire—it was all a little much.

I also happened to share a stormblood with Monty, and

currently had a bright future to look forward to with the Morrigan. Well, no, not exactly *the* Morrigan, but Badb Catha, her scary, blood-chilling side, as some kind of fixer or cleaner or some position that I was sure I would hate.

You could understand my initial hesitation.

"We don't have all night, my Marked One," she said, resting her hand on her hip. "Come. We need to talk."

I didn't recognize her, but something about her voice and the fact that she called me *her* Marked One, gave me a good hint about who was standing before me.

She gave me a slight nod and released some of her energy signature. The unimaginable power signature she possessed washed over me and nearly brought me to my knees.

This was like standing in the vastness of the ocean while mind-numbing waves rose, blotting out the sun and sky as they crested and crashed over me.

"Kali?" I said. "Wait. I'm only seeing two arms carrying no weapons or decapitated heads, and your skin is brown not blue, so I'm guessing, Durga?"

She wore a white, loose-fitting linen blouse, and jeans. Her feet were bare, and she wasn't exactly touching the street with her feet, but instead, hovering slightly above it.

A clear indicator that she wasn't human.

I know—my powers of detection are off-the-charts.

Her jet-black hair was adorned with gold and ivory accents. Over the center of her forehead sat a golden disc, smaller than the last time we met. In the center of that disc sat a softly glowing amethyst, its violet light shining in the night.

Her wrists and ankles were covered with golden bracelets that jingled as she took a few steps away from the Dark Goat. What rushed back to me were her eyes. Her eyes blazed with a piercing violet light, matching the jewel resting on her forehead.

All around me, I heard the familiar birdsong, but it was the middle of the night. All the birds in the city would be sleeping at this hour.

"You guess correctly," she said, her voice melodious. "Come, walk with me."

FIVE

"On this plane, right?" I asked. "We're not leaving the city, are we?"

"No," she said with a short laugh. "Walk with me along *this* street. On *this* plane."

"Just making sure," I said, glancing around and realizing that everything and everyone around me was frozen in time. "*Walk with me* can have many definitions."

"You're learning, that's good."

I cautiously approached her, and glanced back at the Dark Goat.

"They will be secure," she continued. "Nothing will happen to them while we are speaking."

"What about after we finish our conversation?" I asked. "Will that Demogre suddenly appear because we've been frozen in time and it caught up?"

"An excellent question," she said with a nod and a mischievous smile. "Would you like it to?"

I stared at her as if she was insane, then reminded myself who I was giving a stink-eye to, and I quickly modified my stare.

"No," I said quickly. "I would prefer it stay away indefinitely."

"You know that's unrealistic," she said with a shake of her head. "You have enemies, powerful enemies befitting my Marked One. They will not rest until they kill you. Or you them."

"Or you pass this mantle of markedness to someone else?"

She gazed at me for a few seconds, before shaking her head again.

"Do you realize there are multitudes who would *kill* for my Mark?"

"Yes, I'm aware, I've even met a few."

"Yet you wish to discard my favor?"

"I think the word *favor* is stretching it a bit," I said. "Yes, thank you for the curse. I can't believe I'm thanking you for a *curse*. But it *has* kept me alive when I should have been turned to paste and dust several times over."

"You are welcome."

"However, the curse is also responsible for attracting the enemies that were looking to turn me to dust in the first place," I added. "So, there's also that."

"Partly, yes," she said after a pause. "I'd say the majority of the other part was your mouth and attitude."

"I never would have entered this world if it wasn't for your curse."

"Incorrect," she said, looking at me. "When we met, you were not cursed and you were neck deep in a situation that took place in *this world* as you call it."

It was my turn to pause.

She was right.

"Fair enough," I admitted. "I should have never taken that case."

"Hindsight is always clear-eyed and wise," she said. "I'm sure you're wondering why I'm here."

"That entrance could have been less heart-stopping," I said. "You could have just called out my name, or stopped the Dark Goat."

"I could have, but then what is the fun in that?"

"Your concept of fun is very different from mine," I said. "I thought I was going to kill you, well, before I knew who you were."

"Your concern is touching," she said. "But even at the height of your power as my Marked, you would be unable to achieve my death."

"Not literally—nevermind," I said. "Why are you here? Don't gods and goddesses, believe in phones?"

"I suppose I could point out how your words will lead to your early demise, but seeing as how I cursed you alive, it would seem I am somewhat responsible for your attitude."

I shook my head.

"No," I said, "that's all on me. The attitude was in place long before we met, but thanks for admitting you may have had something to do with my wonderful and charming character."

We walked down Centre Street, which was missing traffic and pedestrians, a virtual impossibility in this city at most times.

"You're doing this, aren't you? The lack of people and cars?"

"I'm not actually doing anything," she said, glancing around. "I've merely placed us in the interstice of moments."

"The *and* between one and two?"

"An apt metaphor, yes," she said, admiring the buildings. "I am here because you have several dangerous enemies working in concert to bring about your demise."

"Usually I call that Tuesday," I said. "What makes this so extra dangerous?"

"While your nonchalance is admirable, you would do well

to heed my words," she said. "The Blood Hunter is the least of your problems."

"You can't be serious—she just unleashed one of those demon ogres on us," I said, pointing behind us toward Elk Street. "Monty was freaking out about it. Monty does *not* freak out, and this thing has him panicked. Now you're saying she isn't the worst of my problems?"

"Dira is tracking you."

"Dira is always tracking me, that's not new," I said.

"The Marked of Kali must be tested."

"Couldn't you make it a written test?"

"No, you must undergo trial by fire, as all Marked have done," she said, giving me a look. "It would seem she has acquired a new weapon."

"A new weapon?" I asked, suddenly concerned. "What new weapon?"

"It is named *Chandra* and is what you call a kamikira," she said. "This weapon was given to her by the Blood Hunter you call Esti."

"When did Esti get a kamikira?" I asked. "Where did she get one?"

"Your enemy stole this sword from Iris, who leads my Blades."

"Excuse me, what?"

"The Blades of Kali are a group of fearsome warriors I chose to fight on my behalf," she said. "Iris, their leader, was gifted a special blade—*Chandra*—created to slay gods."

"Why would you, a goddess, give her a god-killer?"

"Did I not say the Blades fight my battles?" she said. "Who do you think they battle—humans?"

"Good point. How did Esti get this Chandra?"

"I would imagine the same way she managed to take hold of a Demogre," Kali said. "Subterfuge, conniving, dark alliances, and thievery."

I nodded.

"Sounds like Esti," I said. "Why give this blade to Dira?"

"Think, Simon," she said, tapping my forehead. "What does she gain by giving this weapon to Dira? What does Dira want more than anything else?"

"To be the Marked of Kali."

"Has she been successful in this endeavor?"

"Not for lack of trying," I said. "She's dangerous."

"All successors are, now she is the most dangerous successor alive," Kali said. "I am here to give you a task."

"What task?"

"Return Chandra to Iris," she said. "She has stayed her hand at my request, but she grows weary of waiting. She wants to lash out and destroy this world for taking what she rightfully earned."

"Overreact much?" I said. "She needs to destroy the entire world just to get her sword back? Maybe if she took better care of it, Esti wouldn't have stolen it from her."

"I strongly urge you to never utter those words in her presence," Kali said with a smile. "Her shame is the only reason she has stayed her hand. She realizes that the Blood Hunter deceived her and managed to steal her weapon, with some help."

"Esti is moving in some powerful circles these days."

"Not her, the Order she currently serves," Kali clarified. "You must be wary of them, they too seek your destruction."

"It seems to be a common thread in my life."

"That is the life of the Marked of Kali," she said, and I resisted the urge to comment on how often she reminded me, avoiding certain pain. "One day—if you live long enough—you will learn to accept it."

"Is that why you came as Durga? To offer protection and strength?"

"I came in this iteration to offer you something other than death and destruction, if you are willing."

"So far this entire conversation has been about how the Kill Simon Fan Club has upgraded their weapons," I said. "What else are you offering, because all I'm seeing is death and destruction headed my way."

"You have a choice as does the mage," she said. "Spilling blood, is, of course, one option."

"You want me to reason with Dira?" I asked in disbelief. "She's fanatically irrational about being the next Marked of Kali, which if you recall, requires that she retire the *current* Marked of Kali."

"And now with Chandra, she actually can," Kali said, stopping at the intersection of Centre Street and Canal Street. "Are you going to let her kill you now that death is a real option?"

"Premature death is not on the agenda, no."

"Do you know why you are immortal?" she asked out of the blue. "Do you know why I cursed you alive?"

"Is that a rhetorical question?" I asked. "*You* cursed me alive and made me your Marked. You don't know?"

She smiled and my blood froze.

The fact that she appeared normal occasionally fooled my brain into answering in normal Simon mode, which meant answers like the one I just gave.

Those answers could get me killed.

Literally.

"What I meant was, no," I said, seriously. "Was that a rhetorical question designed to make me search for the deeper philosophical meaning behind the action?"

"That is not an answer, and no, the questions are not rhetorical."

"I don't know, not really," I said. "How could I imagine what goes on in your mind? I'm not a god."

"That is a good start," she said. "Here are some other questions to set you on the path, should you choose to follow it. Why would the Blood Hunter steal Chandra, only to give it to Dira? Why not use it herself?"

"I don't understand that move either," I said. "Esti hates me with a passion. If she finally had a blade that could kill me, I can't see her not using it."

"She gave Dira a god-killer, and unleashed a Demogre on you and the mage," she said. "Did you tell her you were immortal?"

"That's not exactly the kind of information I like to share."

"It would appear she is acting with that contingency in mind," she said. "Killing an immortal is easy...once you know how."

"How did she find out I was immortal?"

"That is the real question you must answer," she said, placing a hand on my chest. "We will speak again soon."

She pushed gently and I found myself inside the Dark Goat again as we skidded to a stop in the street.

"Did you hit her?" Monty demanded. "Where is she?"

He jumped out of the car.

"She's not there," I said. "You're not going to find her."

"What are you talking about?" he said, whirling on me. "There was a woman in the middle of the street!"

I explained what happened and he calmed down.

"Are you certain?" he asked. "You weren't just hallucinating the entire situation to cope with the fact that you recklessly crushed a woman to death with the car?" He looked around. "A woman I'm currently not seeing lying dead in the street?"

"First of all, I'm not reckless, and no, I didn't hallucinate anything," I said as we jumped back into the Dark Goat. "We need to get somewhere I can ask some questions. I think Esti knows about the curse."

"Did you bother to ask Kali how Esti is tracking you?"

"No, but I think I have an idea," I said. "Something she said leads me to believe Dira is helping her somehow."

"That would make sense," he said. "Dira *can* track you because she's a successor, correct?"

"Correct," I said. "She followed us to London if you recall."

"True," he said, rubbing his chin. "If she's working with Esti, she can relay your position and Esti can ambush us—"

"When we least expect it."

"I believe that's why it's called an ambush," Monty said. "We need to get to Haven. I think we can find someone to ask your questions to there."

"In Haven?" I asked, curious. "You don't mean Roxanne, do you?"

"No, and I don't mean Haven exactly either," he said. "The person I have in mind isn't in Haven but rather under it, in the detention area."

"That's not funny, Monty."

"It wasn't intended to be," he said. "The person we need to see regarding the Demogre and your questions is currently being detained beneath Haven."

"You're serious?"

"Deadly serious, let's go."

SIX

Monty pulled out his phone, dialed Roxanne put the call on speaker as I sped up Centre Street.

"Tristan, who's hurt?" Roxanne said. "What happened? How many injured?"

"You do realize I'm capable of calling you without it being a dire emergency or anyone being injured?" Monty said. "I'm just calling because—"

"Someone died?" she asked, cutting him off. "Who or what tried to kill you? What are you facing this time? You two really need a vacation, somewhere off-plane where nothing is trying to kill you."

Monty took a slow breath.

"No one has been killed—not yet," Monty said. "Esti is back."

"Esti?" Roxanne said. "Did you say Esti? The Blood Hunter?"

"Yes," Monty said. "I wanted you to hear it from me first."

"Hey, Roxanne," I said. "How are things at Haven?"

"Intact," she said. "Tell me you three are not visiting."

"I'm afraid we must," Monty said. "Esti has unleashed a Demogre."

There was a long silence.

It was long enough to make it appear that Roxanne had hung up.

"Roxanne?" Monty said. "Did you hear—?"

"I heard," she said, her voice tight. "Esti is not a mage or sorceress. How did she manage this?"

"We don't know yet," he said. "It may have something to do with the new Order she joined."

"It's impossible," she said, her voice hard. "Demogres were wiped out after the war. Is it possible you misclassified a creature you encountered?"

"I do not misclassify creatures," Monty said. "It was a Demogre."

"I don't mean to offend you, Tristan, so please don't take it that way," she said. "If you and Simon had come across a Demogre, a *real* Demogre, and engaged with it, you wouldn't be calling to tell me about it. I'd be on my way to recover your remains."

"I never said we engaged it in battle," Monty said. "Once I realized what it was, we took the only option open to us."

"We ran," I said. "It was more of a strategic retreat in a strict tactical sense."

"Demogres are lethal mage killers," she said. "It's what they were created for. You wouldn't be able to cast, much less fight one."

"I'm well aware of what they were created for," Monty said as his voice trailed off into his memory. After a few seconds, he snapped back to the present. "I was there when they first unleashed them, did you forget?"

"I've tried to," she said. "Demogres are horrific, unrelenting, monsters of death. How did Esti get ahold of one?"

"I can only assume the Heretics of the Sanguinary Order

have a powerful Bestiarist Mage in their ranks, along with an accomplished summoner," he said. "It's the only way to produce a Demogre that I'm aware of and one of the reasons why we're paying you a visit."

"A what?" I asked. "What kind of mage?"

"Mages who create and experiment on creatures like ogres, trollgres and Demogres are called Bestiarists," Monty said. "It's a long-lost and rarely practiced art for obvious reasons. All of the Councils agreed that no mage should invest any time in creating these creatures or any variation of them."

"They banned the teachings in every magical community," Roxanne added. "But there are still pockets where the Council's authority doesn't reach or is lax."

"That would explain the Demogre," I said. "Esti was waiting for it. She created that trap just for us, well, me. Someone, one of these beasty mages, must have created it."

"That's why I feel it's unlikely," Roxanne said. "You can't simply *create* a Demogre. It's an incredibly complicated process. A demon of sufficient power must be summoned, trapped and enslaved. Then that demon is merged with an ogre of immense power."

"That sounds like all kinds of horrible," I said. "Is that the only way?"

"The only way as far as I know," Roxanne said. "Mages always die in the process of a Demogre formation…Always."

"Why would the Order create one, if it's that risky?" I asked.

"Because they can," Monty said. "That's like asking why humans are so destructive? It's part of our nature."

"Some of us are more destructive than others," I said, shooting him a glance. "Just thought I'd point that out."

"Point taken," he said. "Roxanne, we're headed to you, I also think Simon is being tracked, somehow. Esti knew exactly where we would be and was able to intercept. We need to see him."

"See?" Roxanne asked suddenly guarded. "Who exactly?"

"Salius," Monty continued. "I know you're holding him."

The line went silent.

"Did she just hang up?" I asked. "Who is Salius?"

Monty held up a hand, requesting I remain silent. Roxanne returned a few seconds later.

"How do you come to have that information?" Roxanne asked. "No one except the highest clearance personnel know of his presence at Haven. Where did you learn of this?"

"I'm not at liberty to say," Monty said. "But I can guarantee you it's not a breach of your security."

"Tristan, we need to have a discussion about where you get your information," Roxanne said. "In the meantime, you'll want to go to the Detention Wing."

"So, I can speak to him?"

"Assuming you're dealing with a Demogre, a *true* Demogre, what other alternatives do you have?"

"I am, I just didn't think you would be open to my request."

"Why not?" she asked. "How did you think you were going to get to him without my approval?"

"You are a stickler for rules and regulations—"

"Because they have a tendency to keep people alive!" she snapped. "It's true, you don't have the clearance necessary, but I can make an executive exception because of your status, provided your visit includes a security team."

"Can Simon accompany me?" Monty asked. "Can you facilitate it?"

"I can, but I have to warn you, Salius is still dangerous, even with the runic detainment. How long do you need with him?"

"Long enough to corroborate the proper formation of a Demogre and how to destroy one."

"He *will* know how to create one, but the chances of him sharing how to undo a Demogre is slim," she said. "He's been kept away from magical society, *all* society, for some time. He's not going to be pleasant company."

"Are you saying he's become antisocial?"

"I'm saying he's become violently antisocial," she said. "Besides me, only one other person is authorized to visit him."

"One person?" I asked. "This Salius is that dangerous?"

"Yes, he's that dangerous."

"We'll take our chances—even one of the two answers will help us."

"I'll get the security team ready," she said. "Please arrive at the receiving area in the Detention Wing, first level."

"He's on the first level?" I asked, still slightly confused. "Wouldn't someone that dangerous be placed in a more secure area?"

"That's where we're meeting," Roxanne clarified. "We're going to the Well—one of the deepest sub-levels in Haven where he's housed. I hope neither of you are claustrophobic. His quarters aren't exactly expansive."

"We'll make do," Monty said. "We also need to scan Simon. I think his signature has shifted and he's being tracked."

"Tracked? By whom?"

"Esti," he said. "She was able to find him with enough ease to set up an effective trap."

"I can do that personally."

"We should be there in ten minutes," he said. "Can we get the scan before we see him?"

"Yes, I hope you're certain about this," she said. "See you then."

She ended the call.

"I thought you knew how to fight a Demogre?" I said as we raced uptown. "Why do you need to meet with this Demogre expert?"

"I'm not an expert on demonology or creatures of this type," Monty said, glancing out of the window. "He is both and possesses valuable information."

"Will he share that information with us?"

"That depends on how cooperative he's feeling," Monty said after a moment. "He is brilliantly deranged, and, as Roxanne said, quite dangerous."

"If this Salius is detained, how is he dangerous?"

"He's a darkmage, a powerful one who rose up the ranks of the Golden Circle Elders before anyone discovered his true nature," Monty said. "He may be reluctant to share anything with me particularly."

"Why?"

"It was my uncle who discovered his immersion in darkness and put a stop to it," he said. "My uncle nearly killed him in the process."

"*Nearly* killed him?"

SEVEN

"Salius Montague is a distant relative who possesses a gift for creating what we call…monsters."

"Montague?" I asked, surprised. "He's related to you?"

"My family is quite large," Monty said matter-of-factly. "You've only met a small, mostly unhinged portion of it. Don't forget, the Montagues formed a large part of the Golden Circle. We figured prominently in its foundation for good…and bad."

"Who is Salius to you?"

"Distant," he said. "He's my grandfather's brother, which makes him my great uncle. Thankfully, he's not as strong as Uncle Dexter. That would be problematic, considering his propensity for creature creations."

"Dexter stopped him…but managed *not* to kill him?"

"Contrary to popular belief, my uncle doesn't go around murdering his relatives."

"But it *was* Dex who stopped Salius."

"The one and same," he said. "Mostly for his own good. Salius's experiments were getting increasingly out of hand and

Haven was the only place equipped, until recently to house him safely."

"He's a danger to himself?"

"He's a danger to everyone around him," Monty said, shaking his head. "You recall my mentioning Bestiarists?"

"Yes, the mages who can create ogres and monsters?"

"Salius is one of the most accomplished bestiarists to exist," he said. "The only problem is he believes in setting his creatures free in the world, and that no creature should live in captivity. You can imagine the kind of problem that might create."

"I can see where that would be dangerous," I said, imagining all sorts of creatures roaming the streets of the city. "Actually, that would be bad. Can you trust him?"

"He's family. He may be deranged, but I can trust him with my life," Monty said. "He lives for a challenge. Being detained in Haven, I'm certain he's starved for mental stimulation. I simply have to present the correct type of challenge and bait to gain his cooperation."

"From the way Roxanne described him, this sounds like a horrible idea," I said. "You sure you want to see him?"

"Salius is not deranged, well maybe slightly, but he's not antisocial or violent," Monty explained. "He is, however, different and maybe a little quirky. She doesn't know him like I do."

"I hope you're right."

"You'll see."

We pulled up into the Haven parking lot.

"You're going to use the Demogre as the challenge?"

"That and his freedom," Monty said. "I can't just mention the Demogre, I have to offer to let him see it...in person."

"In *person*?" I asked. "Isn't Roxanne going to have some words about that? Violent words, like 'no' and 'over my dead body' and 'hell no'?"

"Yes, they will be mostly angry ones, which is why I'm not going to share that part with her," he said. "Not yet, not while we're still on the premises."

"Which part do you think is going to upset her more?" I asked. "The part where you bribe Salius with his freedom, or the part where you break him out of prison to go see a monster?"

"All of it," Monty said, his voice hard. "I need you to back me on this, Simon. It's true, Salius is a danger if released, but the danger he poses, pales in comparison to the Demogre, and there's more."

"More worse? Of course there is worse. What's worse?"

"Whoever created that Demogre may be capable of creating more creatures," Monty said. "Some even more dangerous than the Demogre."

"Okay, that sounds worse."

"You have no idea," he said. "I'm hoping I can appeal to Salius's sense of duty to set this right. Fundamentally, he is a mage of duty and honor. I know he will do the right thing."

"How? By telling him there's a monster loose and only he can help us stop it? Thin, Monty…razor thin."

"Yes, but it will spur him into action."

"This Salius is in this Well, which sounds like the equivalent of a supermax for mages," I said. "It almost sounds like you want us to break him out?"

"Not break him out exactly, just out for a short walkabout until we stop the Demogre," he said as if he made any kind of sense. "Then if he wants, he can go back to the Well."

"If he *wants*?"

"There *are* alternatives to the Well."

"You've lost your mind," I said, glancing at him. "Are you listening to yourself right now? You want to go up against Roxanne and her security force? Elias is almost as dangerous as Roxanne, if not *just* as dangerous with his crew of sorcerer security agents."

"We won't have to face them," he said. "I have a plan. No one will get hurt."

"You have a *plan*?" I asked, incredulous. "A plan to get us *killed*?"

"We do have to be careful about how we go about this," Monty said. "They must not uncover our ruse."

"When did this become 'we'?" I asked. "I don't want to go up against an angry Roxanne or Elias Paul Bunyan. He may be a sorcerer, but he's built like a powerlifter. How long have you had this plan?"

"The plan has existed for some time," Monty said. "The Demogre is the perfect cover. Salius is the only one who can assist us in this."

"You mean get us killed. This can go wrong in so many ways," I said, shaking my head. "Why not just ask Roxanne? I'm sure you can convince her."

"There are many things I admire about Roxanne," he said. "But she would never agree to releasing Salius. He's a dangerous mage."

"A dangerous *darkmage*," I corrected. "You left out the dark part."

"There's more, but I can't divulge that until I know you're on board," he said. "Will you do it?"

"Of course, I'll do it," I said. "Like you have to ask. However, I'm claiming plausible deniability and filing a formal protest. That way when Roxanne blasts you, I get to say I told you so."

He breathed out a sigh of relief as if there was a chance I would refuse. There *was* a chance I would refuse if he were about to commit some unforgivable act of darkness, I mean I did have some limits, but this was Monty.

If he was asking for help, I was going to help.

Even if it meant breaking out some distant darkmage relative out of maximum security detention, and angering probably the most powerful sorceress I knew.

"We're going to die, aren't we?"

"Don't be so cynical," he said. "I *do* have this figured out, and this is for the greater good."

"That's what worries me," I said. "You have this figured out. You have an exfil from Haven's Detention Center as one of your contingency plans. Did you plan on being kept there someday?"

"I try to plan for every eventuality," he said. "It's what a—"

"Good mage does, yes, I know," I finished. "Does Dex know about this?"

"As I said, there's more, but I can't share it here," he said, glancing around Haven, and concerning me even more. "Suffice to say there are other factors at play."

"Are you saying Dex knows?"

"I'm saying that the situation regarding Salius has changed recently, precipitating a relocation of his living quarters."

"Which sounds like Dex doesn't know."

"Don't worry, as I said, I have a plan," he assured me. "Of course, you will have to play along as my clueless assistant until we facilitate his short vacation from Haven. He must not perceive you as a threat."

"Clueless in the magical world—that won't be too much of a stretch, and I can do harmless," I said. "What about Peaches? Won't he know Peaches is a hellhound, being a creature expert?"

"There is that," he said as we stepped out of the Dark Goat. My hellhound bounded out, rocking the car as he walked over to my side and nearly crushed one of my toes. with his stone paws. "You will have to create a convincing backstory for how you ended up with him."

"*I* have to create it?"

"It will sound more authentic if you do it," he said. "That way you can add your own personal touch. Maybe something involving saving Corbel's life and Hades repaying you by gifting you a hellhound pup?"

"That can work," I said, rubbing my chin as we approached Haven. "You think Roxanne has some anxiety about us visiting?"

"I would if I were her," he said with a nod. "Every time we visit this facility, I'm replacing equipment. The expenses have been staggering. I had no idea the equipment they use in the Medical Wing were could be so costly."

"Equipment or the facility itself, like that time Evers decided to redo that bridge?" I said. "Or when that ogre smashed through a floor?"

He pinched the bridge of his nose.

"Please, let's not relive those not-so-pleasant memories, thank you."

"We don't plan it that way," I said, looking up at Haven's newly renovated Medical Wing. "It's not our fault our enemies like to come at us while we're in Haven."

"Technically, it *is* our fault," Monty said as we approached a ramp that led to the Detention Wing. "If we visited less often, they would have to attack us at other locations."

"Besides, you have to see your lady," I said. "We have to visit as often as possible. You don't want her getting cranky because you're not paying her enough attention. That would be no bueno."

"We can't visit more," he said, gazing around the complex. "My presence here attracts the wrong element to Roxanne's location. Pirn is here and can keep Haven safe, but some of the beings seeking her are beyond Elias. The less I'm here, the better."

"I doubt she sees it that way," I said. "The more you're here, the more you can keep an eye on things."

"I don't know if you've noticed, but Roxanne does not prefer a micromanagement style, unless she's the one doing the micromanaging."

"I'm just saying that you should spend more time on dates and outings," I said. "It will keep your relationship fresh and spontaneous, know what I mean?"

"Am I to believe that you want me to take relationship advice from an immortal dating—what is for all intents and purposes—another immortal, who subsists on blood?"

"I'll admit it's not what's considered an average relationship—"

"Didn't she try to kill you the last time you two 'spoke'?"

"Not really, she was just proving a point, by showing me that she could," I said. "It was a demonstration of ability."

"Of course, that sounds quite fresh and spontaneous, like a sudden death is fresh and spontaneous," he said. "This is the same reason why we can't visit Haven often. Haven't you noticed the paradox?"

"What paradox?"

"For someone who is so long-lived, like me, and a cursed alive immortal, like you, we certainly attract plenty of death wherever we go," he said. "*This* is why Haven gets attacked."

"Your logic is broken," I said, shaking my head. "They're not attacking us because we're at Haven, they're attacking us because of who we are, not where we are."

He stared at me for a few seconds and then shook his head.

"That's *exactly* what I just said," he said. "Never mind, will your creature adjust to going deep underground?"

"I have to think he'll be okay," I said, glancing at Peaches who padded silently next to me. "I mean his dad comes from a place literally called the Underworld, I'm going to say he's going to be okay being in a deep underground space. How about you?"

"I've been to the Well before," he said. "It's unexpected. I suggest you brace yourself."

"I've been to Haven before," I said. "Remember when you were having your episode?"

"It was not an *episode*, it was a schism," he said. "I was going through a shift."

We pushed through the door at the bottom of the ramp.

"Sure looked like an episode to me," I answered. "Anyway, we were down here then, to deal with your non-episode mage schism."

We stepped into a large reception area and were immediately surrounded by Pirn Security.

At first I thought they were all mages, but their signatures were different, slightly off from what I associated with mages. It made sense. If Elias was recruiting and leading this group, he wouldn't bring mages to his team, he would bring in sorcerers like him.

It also seemed like Elias was recruiting from the nearest sorcerer gym. Most of the agents around us spent time lifting heavy things up and putting them down again.

"These guys look serious," I said, keeping my hands away from my holster. "Looks like Elias has been on a hiring spree. I don't remember that many security personnel when you were here as Roxanne's guest. Are they all sorcerers?"

Monty gave me one short nod.

I raised my hands slowly.

"We come in peace," I said as none of them so much as cracked a smile. I glanced at Monty. "Tough crowd."

"Good evening, sirs," one of the younger security members said and stepped forward. "We're here to escort you to the Director and Mr. Pirn, who will be leading the team to the Well. It's an honor to be your escort for this operation."

"Operation?" I said and looked at Monty again, who shook his head at me. "This op have a name?"

"Yes, sir. It does."

He failed to produce the name, probably because I failed to ask for it. Many of these security types were ex-military, and most of those had a tendency to be literal about things, like names and providing information.

These agents had the added bonus of being low to mid-level sorcerers. I could sense their energy signatures and realized that alone, Monty and I could handle any one of them. Together—and I counted easily twenty of them—they could be a force to be reckoned with, if they worked as a cohesive unit.

Knowing Elias, he had this team operating like a well-oiled machine of security and destruction, if need be.

There was no scenario where I wanted to test their level of destruction... and Monty was planning to break out his great uncle.

If we made a mistake, this was going to hurt. A lot.

"What's your name?" I asked the team member. "Looks like Elias left you as point in his absence."

"Yes, sir," he said. "Name is Taggart, sir."

This team looked structured, but I knew Elias wasn't a hardass. He was tough but fair, and he would give his men some latitude.

I outstretched a hand.

"I'm Simon Strong," I said and we clasped hands. "You can call me Strong. The angry-looking mage over there is Monty, but everyone calls him Mr. Cranky to his face."

Monty scowled in my direction and nodded at Taggart.

Some of the security team behind Taggart smiled, hid their faces, or looked away to hide smiles.

"We've been briefed on who you are," Taggart said. "Simon Strong and Tristan Montague. Pleasure to meet you both. If you would come with us, we'll escort you to the Director and our Team Leader."

"This here is Peaches," I said, rubbing my hellhound's massive head. "He looks dangerous, and is really a ferocious hellhound. Unless you happen to have some sausage? Then he's less ferocious and more on the starving side. Right, boy?"

I rubbed Peaches's head and belly again.

"Peaches," Taggart said with a nod. "Direct scion of Cerberus and a huge fan of meat? He'd fit right in with some of us on the team. Pirn calls us Haven's Hellhounds."

I noticed all of the men had a patch on the left shoulder of a large, canine—looking creature that closely resembled my own hellhound. The hellhound on the patch was in mid-leap, breathing fire from its mouth, and had blazing, red eyes.

"I like the patch," I said. "Close resemblance."

"Thanks. We had it made after watching some of the past security footage. Did you want one?" Taggart asked. "Being considered a Hellhound is the highest honor for our teams. Would it be okay if I gave him some meat?"

"Yes," I said, "After all, meat is—"

"Life," Taggart finished. "We know."

I nodded, mildly surprised as Taggart reached into a front pocket and pulled out a large rolled up sausage. He looked at me first before offering it to my ever-voracious hellhound. I nodded. He held it out, and Peaches gently removed the sausage from Taggart's fingers lightly with his teeth.

"You guys *were* well-briefed."

"Yes, sir."

I glared at my hellhound and shook my head.

"When I offer you a sausage, you usually try to take my arm off, you ham," I said. "But you take his sausage as nice as you please. What gives?"

Peaches devoured the sausage in one chomp and I could tell that one action impressed most of the team, causing some nods of approval from them. I figured this was probably their first experience with a hellhound, even though they were sorcerers and used to seeing the extraordinary.

Some of them even took a few steps closer to get a better look at Peaches. It was the first time I had seen my hellhound create an environment of acceptance among a group.

<You heard him. Being a hellhound is the highest honor. He speaks truth. Maybe one day they can be mighty too.>

<You could have been a little ferocious.>

<He offered the meat nicely and I didn't want to scare him. Do you want me to smile? I can be friendly too.>

He unleashed a thousand-watt smile, which looked like he was on the verge of chewing off one of Taggart's arms.

<Don't smile at them. They'll get scared. Just thank him for the sausage, but not too loud.>

Peaches let out a low rumble which reverberated through the floor and cracked half a smile at Taggart who bravely stood his ground in front of Peaches.

"Wow, that was loud. If...if you'll join us, we'll head down," Taggart said, turning and leading the group to a large door, where the men could walk shoulder to shoulder five at a time. He pointed at the large, rune-covered metal door. "This way, please."

I motioned forward.

"Lead the way."

EIGHT

The large door led to a long, rune-covered corridor that sloped gradually downward.

At the bottom of this corridor was another door. This one looked robust. It appeared to be borrowed from a bank, complete with a large wheel and turning arm.

"That door looks secure," I said. "Last line of defense?"

"I'm not allowed to divulge that information, sir," Taggart said. "But it's meant to be a hard stop to anything that wants to get out that's not supposed to."

"Get out?" I asked. "Not get in?"

"No one and nothing wants to get *into* Haven, sir."

They continued walking ahead and I hung back a bit with Monty. They gave us room, but they kept us within the larger circle formed by the team as we all moved forward.

"That door looks major," I said under my breath to Monty. "Did you do those runes?"

Monty shook his head as he examined the runes from a distance.

"No. These are sorcerous runes, which differ considerably from the runes I would use," he said. "Mine are more like deterrents with some lethal consequences, depending on the level of severity and the depth of a breach."

"And these?"

He stepped forward slightly and peered closer at the runes.

"These have no ramp-up," he said. "They go from one minor warning to disintegration or maiming. You don't want to try these runes in any of their iterations."

"The purpose of a detention center is to keep the inhabitants inside," he continued. "Haven is very effective at doing this."

I gazed at the softly glowing red runes on the door.

"Your woman can be pretty scary sometimes."

"I only have two words for you," Monty said. "Reaping Wind."

"Fair enough," I said with a nod as Taggart swung the massive door open, and most of the team filed in. Three of the team remained outside the door, standing guard. "Both our ladies are scary."

"I have no idea what you're referring to," Monty said as Taggart closed the door. Standing behind it was a determined-looking Roxanne. "Hello, Roxanne."

"Hello, Roxanne," I said nearly choking on the rest of my words. "It's good to see you there standing behind the door."

"You were saying something about being scary?" she asked. "You do know this entire facility is equipped with a state of the art wireless intercom system that can be set to passive voice activation?"

"No wonder the team was silent on the way down here," I said, glancing at the security team around me. "I'm guessing they knew."

"Don't say anything you don't want overheard," Elias said from behind one of the larger team members. "Hello, Strong, Mr. Montague. It's good to see you both."

"Tristan, please," Monty said. "After all, you did to make sure I recovered well during my brief stay at Haven."

Elias nodded as I stepped back and noticed he had clearly been spending time in the gym—actually, he looked like he had been spending some time *lifting* the gym.

"Are you actually larger than the last time I saw you?" I asked. "You trying to generate your own gravitational field?"

"All my agents have to be strong in mind, body and spirit," he said. "Same goes for the Team Leader."

"Lead by example?"

"Precisely. We don't do stereotypical sorcerers at Pirn Security," he said. "Also, I've found a new training partner, and she kicks my rear in the gym."

"She? You found someone insane enough to train with you?"

"Her name is Hanna, and she is quite fierce," he said with a small smile and clapped me on the shoulder. "She speaks highly of you. Something about you finding your battlecry. Care to share that with the team?"

"You train with Nan?" I asked, mildly shocked. "Wait, she lets you call her Hanna?"

"It's her name."

"I know, but she *lets* you call her Hanna?"

His smile grew ever so wider and he subtly wagged his eyebrows.

"She does," he said.

I shook my head in wonder.

Roxanne coughed and he composed himself, the smile disappearing from his face.

"But, we're not here to discuss my training partners," Elias said. "I understand you want to go down to the Well?"

"Yes," Monty said. "I need to see him."

"You realize what you're asking is normally restricted,"

Elias said. "Sal is a great guy but he doesn't get visitors. In fact, he's only allowed one visitor."

"Sal?" I asked. "Are you're on a first name basis with all the prisoners?"

"Salius is not a prisoner," Elias said. "He is a guest."

"He can leave whenever he wants?" I asked, irked at the semantics. "Are you saying he can head out the front door at any time?"

"No," Elias answered. "You don't understand."

"Clarify it for me then."

"When the Well was created for him, it was with the understanding that it could only hold one occupant," Elias said. "His ability—do you even know his ability?"

"He's a Bestiarist."

"Yes and no," Elias said. "He's a Bestiarist, the same way Michelangelo was a sculptor or Einstein was smart. Technically those definitions fit, but they don't describe the depth and brilliance of the person."

"He's a gifted Bestiarist?"

"The reason he's in Haven is because he's losing control of his skill, his ability, so to speak," Elias explained. "If he's placed in an unruned, neutral environment, he can create a creature almost by accident."

"What?" I asked. "What do you mean by accident?"

"I mean it takes little thought and almost no effort on his part to create a creature," Elias said. "Most of the ones that appear are benign. He didn't require specialized housing until the razor-backed panther became defensive and tried to kill some of my agents."

"The razor-backed what?" I asked. "It tried to kill…did you say razor-backed panther?"

"All his creatures are very protective of him," he said. "If they feel any form of threat directed toward Sal, they don't ask questions, they go full SEND."

"Seek, Evaluate, and Destroy?"

"They usually skip the middle and jump right to the destroy part," Elias said. "Imagine him, walking around the city or anywhere for that matter, with a menagerie of creatures all primed to shred anyone who a danger to Sal, it would end in sooner rather than later."

"So you imprisoned him?" I asked, turning to Roxanne. "Against his will?"

"No," she said. "Salius Montague, of sound body and mind, voluntarily surrendered to Haven to live in the Well. It's just that his time here, has impacted his mind."

"It's no longer entirely sound," Monty said. "How many will be escorting us to see him?"

"Why do you need to see him?" Elias asked. "I need to state the reason in our records. Is Strong accompanying you?"

"Yes," Monty said. "Would you prefer he remain behind? I thought seeing the hellhound would be good for Salius, seeing as how he's not allowed to create any companions of his own."

"Not a bad idea," Elias said with a short nod before glancing at Peaches. "For obvious reasons, he's not allowed any animal companions, even in a runed environment. We tried that…once. Jerry still has the scars from the oversized mouse that almost took him out. Salius won't be able to manipulate a hellhound's unique genetic structure. Your hellhound should be safe."

Monty nodded.

"Very well," he said, looking at Roxanne. "Are we ready?"

NINE

"Elias you're with me and pick three others," Roxanne said. "The rest of you will be a RARE team on standby, ready to deploy if something goes wrong."

"What could possibly go wrong?" Monty said. "We're in one of the most secure locations in the city."

"Do I need to remind you how many times I've been attacked in one of the most secure locations in the city?" Roxanne asked, then turned to Elias. "Elias, pick your three."

"RARE Team?"

"Rapid Response," Elias said. "First ones in, last ones out."

"Ortiz, Walters, and Baker are with me," Elias said, pointing to each of the men. "Walters, bring the Hammer. Taggart and the rest of you will remain at the staging area as rapid response."

"Yes, sir," they all said as one.

"Specific ordnance, sir?" Taggart asked. "Are we expecting trouble?"

Elias turned to face us.

"You two planning on getting attacked?" Elias asked,

looking at Monty and me. "Nothing personal, our incidents of violence have a tendency to spike when you two decide to pay us a visit."

"No attacks on the agenda," Monty said. "Nothing out of the ordinary at least."

Elias gave him a look and turned to his team.

"Rapid response team be ready for heavy assault, just in case the *agenda* changes," Elias said. "Those coming with me all-general kit. Sal isn't going to be creating anything down there and no one is going to be casting in the Well."

"Yes, sir," they said in unison and began getting prepped.

"That will take a few minutes," Roxanne said, stepping over to the side. "Tristan, you said Simon needs to be scanned?"

"Esti said something that disturbed me," Monty said. "She said: *You can't hide from me, Simon. I can always find you.*"

"Empty bravado?" Roxanne asked. "Something to rattle Simon so he's always on edge?"

"Normally, I would agree," Monty said. "But Dira, his successor, was able to track us to London."

"I'm going to assume that this successor is not friendly?" Roxanne asked. "This *successor* tracked you across an ocean?"

"Yes, she was given this ability by Kali, I think," I said. "Something to make my life interesting."

"Your goddess has a unique interpretation on how to make life interesting," Roxanne said. "What does this successor wants?"

"Me dead," I said. "It's how she can become the Marked of Kali. In order for her to get the title, I have to retire...from life."

"I see," Roxanne said, looking at me and pointing to a nearby chair. "And now this Esti has been able to track you?"

"I don't think so exactly," I said. "I think Esti and Dira are working together or are associated somehow. Esti gave Dira a sword."

"According to whom?"

"Kali."

"Kali told you Esti gave Dira a sword?" Roxanne asked. "She's speaking to you now?"

"Well, not right now, but I am her Marked One—we talk," I said. "Usually she's doing the talking, and I'm trying not to make her homicidal, but yes we talk every so often."

"And Kali informed you that Esti gave Dira a sword to do what?"

"To kill me," I said. "It's a special sword."

"Let me see if I understand what you're saying," Roxanne said. "You spoke to Kali, the goddess Kali—"

"Is that what's hanging you up?" I asked. "Why is that so hard to accept? You and Monty wiggle your fingers and form orbs of energy in your hands, but my speaking to a goddess is suddenly far-fetched?"

"Apologies," she said, raising a hand. "I didn't mean to offend you, it's just that Kali is quite esoteric, and her followers distinguish themselves by their devout worship. Two words I have a hard time associating with you, Simon."

"Well, I don't worship Kali or any god," I said. "They have a horrible track record with me. That doesn't mean we don't speak and that she didn't mark me."

"True," Roxanne admitted, motioning to the back of my hand. "She *has* marked you. Esti stole this special sword to give to Dira, a successor, in order for the successor to kill you? Why not kill you herself? According to Tristan, she unleashed a Demogre on you both."

"That's an excellent question," I said. "If I can get her to stop trying to remove me from existence for a few minutes, I'll make sure to ask her."

"What sword?" Monty asked. "Simon, tell us the name of the sword."

"Oh, the name of the sword is *Chandra*. I'm sure it means something fearsome, like invincible god-slayer or destroyer of enemies."

"What?" Roxanne said, grabbing my arm. "What name did you say?"

"Chandra?" I repeated. "You know this sword?"

"There is only one sword named Chandra that I know of. Actually that is short for Chandrahasa, and it means laughter of the moon. It belongs to a fearsome warrior," Roxanne said, lowering her voice. "If this is the same person I have in mind, you have truly stepped into it this time, Simon."

"Do you mean Iris?" I said, hesitatingly. "She leads the Blades of Kali."

"Bloody hell," she said under her breath as she shook her head. "Yes, the Blades of Kali."

"I want to say they're some new edgy, new-age band, but I'm guessing it's more serious than that," I said. "Judging from your reaction, not a new edgy new age band?"

"Do you know what the Blades of Kali are?" Roxanne asked as fear creeped into her voice. "What they *truly* are?"

"I don't think I want to know. Do I want to know?"

"They are assassins, god-killers," Roxanne clarified. "This is the group tasked with carrying out Kali's, for lack of a better definition, hit jobs."

"Hit jobs?"

"Except that their targets are not humans, they're gods or beings of immense power," Roxanne added. "They are not to be taken lightly."

"And they use Chandra for this?"

"Yes, Chandra is a cursed sword, powerful yes, but cursed. Iris will find this Dira and remove her head."

"What's with the head removal?" I asked. "She can't just ask for her sword back?"

"I suppose she could, but she won't. That's not how the Blades function. They adhere to ancient ways of dealing with insults and affronts."

"You mean they get biblical with justice? Eye for an eye and all that?"

"Exactly. If Esti stole her sword, Iris has lost face," Roxanne said.

"That means taking off Dira's head?"

"It means killing whoever currently wields it," Roxanne said. "It's a matter of honor."

"Wouldn't asking for it back without the whole decapitating thing restore Iris's honor? Granted, there is less blood, but that's a good thing."

"Iris needs to make a statement," Roxanne said. "Dira will be made an example of, and most likely Esti too for stealing it."

"Why not just go after the thief? Dira didn't steal it."

"This *is* the same Dira who wants to kill you, correct?"

"Yes, but she's being set up," I said. "Esti is playing a game here and using her as a pawn somehow."

"And you want to *save* Dira?" Roxanne asked. "Why not let Iris kill Dira? She gets her sword back and you dispatch Esti. Or let her kill them both, which then makes your life easy."

"My life is never that simple."

"In this, we agree. However, most of the complexity that occurs in your life is due to your responses when silence would have been more appropriate, and life-preserving."

"I get that a lot."

"I'm sure," she said with a nod. "Tell me why it's not that simple."

"There's a wrinkle," I said. "I wish it was easier, but Kali wants me to *help* Dira, not kill her—at least not right now. Are you really asking me to explain the convoluted thought process of a goddess?"

"Understood, it can be complicated in the best of times," Roxanne said, raising a hand and looking at Monty. "Tristan, what am I scanning Simon for?"

"Energetic tethers of any kind," Monty said. "I doubt Esti can track at that level, but then again I never thought she could have access to a Demogre. She's getting help, and that concerns me."

"You think it's the Blood Hunters?"

"It's how they hunt down vampires," Monty said. "They use energetic tethers to track them and wait to attack during the day when they are at their weakest. I fear something similar is being used but enhanced somehow, to interact with Dira and whoever created this Demogre."

"Vampires have a particular signature that Simon lacks," she said. "Dira, on the other hand, may present a problem. She may be keyed to Simon's signature due to this whole successor and Marked interaction."

"While true. It doesn't account for Esti having that sword or being able to locate Simon and lay a trap for him so soon after leaving the Hellfire Club," Monty said. "That tracking was too precise."

"This is all being caused by Esti somehow," I said, looking at Roxanne as she approached me. "She's a little upset because I cut off one of her arms and caused her banishment by the Blood Hunters. We've stopped being friends since then."

Roxanne stared at me for a few seconds.

"This is no joking matter, Simon," she said. "The Heretics of the Sanguinary Order, like the Blades of Kali, are a very real threat. Chandra is a fearsome weapon in Iris' hands, and it sounds like this Dira has no trouble finding you if she can track you across an ocean. You need to take these enemies seriously."

"I do."

"Now sit still and let me see if I can figure out how your fan club can find you so easily."

TEN

"Have you recently received any gifts from either Dira or Esti?" she asked as she extended her fingers and spread out her arms in what looked like an imminent hug. "Anything?"

"I don't make it a habit of accepting gifts from people trying to kill me, no matter how nice they ask," I said. "Just a little while ago, Esti was trying really hard to gift me a blood arrow. I politely declined her kind offer."

"The arrow," Roxanne said, looking at Monty. "Did it imprint on him?"

"I don't know," Monty said. "I'm not an expert on blood arrows."

"Did his blood mix or touch any part of the arrow shaft, the part covered in runes?"

"Yes," I said. "It was buried in my arm; I'm going to say it's safe to assume my blood touched it."

"That is how she will find you from that point on," Roxanne said. "With that arrow, she managed to bind a tracking cast to your signature, but that doesn't explain—"

"—how she found me before burying an arrow in my arm," I finished. "Dira?"

"It's the only logical explanation," she said after giving it some thought. "Either Dira informed Esti, or Esti has somehow managed to pinpoint your energy signature. Neither is too far-fetched."

"Excuse me?" I asked. "My energy signature is easy to pinpoint?"

"For one who is trained in tracking arts or is skilled enough, yes."

"Can you expand on that?"

"Well, Dira has an advantage," Roxanne said. "Are there any others hunting you?"

"To my knowledge, no," I said. "But I've discovered that my body of knowledge is severely lacking in this world."

"She is linked to you in ways even I can't understand. Suffice to say, it is unlikely you will ever be able to escape Dira. Unless and until you kill her."

"That I'm prepared for," I said. "Kali said as much, and frankly in a very twisted way, I can understand where Dira is coming from. Esti not so much."

"Hatred is a powerful motivator," Roxanne answered. "You maimed and disfigured her. She holds a deep hatred for you."

"I only made the outside match the inside," I said. "She was maimed and disfigured way before she met me."

"Be that as it may, she's made your death her life's mission," she said. "You've given her purpose, which is a dangerous and powerful thing."

"Wonderful," I said. "I thought, as a Blood Hunter, her purpose was the eradication of all vampires."

"It most likely is twisted up in her mind, due to your feelings for Michiko," Roxanne said. "To Esti, you personify her deepest hatreds, someone who deeply hurt her and who has feelings for the vampire she probably hates the most."

"You do seem to have a knack for making formidable

enemies," Monty said. "If she has access to a Demogre, she's just moved to the top of your 'retire' list, along with whoever helped her access that creature."

"Speaking of, it seems the team is nearly ready," Roxanne said looking over my shoulder. "Now, hold still while I perform this scan."

She whispered some words, and light blue energy covered both of her hands. She kept her arms outstretched and ran them along the length of my body, one hand on either side of me.

The blue energy flowed from her hands and gently enveloped me. The feeling of static electricity covered my body as she moved her hands from the sides of my head down to my feet.

She stood up after performing her scan and gave me an odd look.

"What?" I asked. "What did you sense?"

"You've changed," she said, still giving me that same look. "Usually energy signatures remain constant over a person's life. There may be slight fluctuations, but for the most part, they remain the same."

"And mine?"

"The established bonds you have, your curse, your hellhound, and Tristan through the stormblood, those are all strong," she said. "The others are changing, growing stronger, but they seem to be in flux as if they're evolving."

"Which exactly are growing stronger?"

"You are a set of three within a set of three," she said. "I've never seen anything like it in someone who wasn't magically inclined."

"Can you explain that for the non-magically inclined?"

"Three bonds form a foundation: your curse, signifying your bond to Kali, your hellhound, defining your role as bondmate; and Tristan, defining your brotherhood through the stormblood."

"That all makes sense," I said. "What are the other three bonds?"

"They all stem from your connection to your weapon. There is the bond between you and Michiko, the bond between the necrotic aspect you recently acquired, and the seraphic bond. This is a combination I have never seen. If it wasn't for your curse keeping you alive—"

"I'd be dead already?"

"Well, yes," she said. "There are inherent masks in some of the bonds which make it difficult to locate you, but if the tracker is skilled, or of a high enough level, you're probably one of the easiest signatures to track, once the tracker knows what to look for. You shine like the sun at midnight for the right person."

"And this person is Esti?"

"No," Roxanne said. "She's not strong or powerful enough to track your bonds—not even Dira could, outside of what was allowed to her by Kali. This must be someone else, someone powerful and accomplished."

"Stronger than you?" I asked. "What about Monty?"

"Tristan can't factor in this because he shares a bond with you," she said. "He can find you with ease."

"Whoever is doing this tracking is stronger than me in this respect," she said. "If I had to guess, I would say look in the Sanguinary Order. They are known for using blood magic in arcane and forbidden rituals the Blood Hunters won't attempt. This tracking is dark magic."

"On that topic," Monty said, "we should head to the Well."

"Simon, you need to be careful with this," she said, concern in her voice. "This dark magic has left marks, but they are subtle, almost imperceptible. Whoever this is, is skilled and adept at tracking you."

"Is there any way for me to block them?"

She shook her head slowly.

"You would be better off finding them and eliminating them," she said, her voice hard. "This does not bode well. Anyone trucking in this kind of casting means you harm."

"We're ready, Director," Elias said as he and his group approached where we stood. "Everyone ready to go to the Well?"

"Yes," she said. "Lead the way, Elias."

ELEVEN

We arrived at the door and the runes which looked serious from a distance, but now looked angry, and lethal up close.

"Those are some major runes," I said, making sure not to touch or activate them. "How bad would it be if I tripped them?"

"We'd find out how strong Kali's curse is," Roxanne said. "At first, you'd get a mild shock. After that, if you persisted, you'd get a life-ending blast of dark energy. After that—"

"After that?" I asked surprised. "The life-ending blast isn't enough?"

"Not everything is stopped by one blast of energy," she explained. "After that, the entire ramp converts into a nullification zone." She swept an arm up the ramp, causing the floor, walls, and ceiling to burst to life with more of the same angry runes. "This being the only way in or out means there's no escape."

"And no hope," I said, looking at the ramp of death. "What if they survive that?"

"If whatever is trying to escape survives that, it means we are all dead or soon to be," she said, her voice hard.

The runes faded out.

"So this is the only way in and out?" I said, keeping my face neutral and not looking at Monty. "Makes controlling access easy."

"It was designed that way," Elias said. "The same with the Pit."

"The what? Excuse me, did you say, the Pit?" I asked and turned to Roxanne. "You have a Pit?"

She nodded and Elias answered.

"There is another level below the Well," Elias said. "Far below the Well. We won't be going anywhere near that today, thankfully. It takes several layers of clearance and vetting to get past security."

"I wasn't aware the Pit was operational," Monty said nonchalantly, but I knew the tone. It was his 'this is a red flag, but I will act like it's not that important' tone. This Pit concerned him enough to ask the question as he brushed off his sleeve, which meant it *really* concerned him. "Since when? I thought it wouldn't be used for another decade or so?"

"It's not exactly operational," Elias said with a slight cough. "The crews are still inscribing the layers of extinction runes—you know how dangerous that can be."

"Extinction runes?" I asked. "As in—?"

"Yes," Elias said. "Extinction runes don't need explanation. If you run afoul of them, you end up extinct. Simple and brutal."

"How dangerous are they to inscribe?"

"One miscalculation and you lose the inscriber and his entire team," Monty said. "Inscribers of that caliber are difficult to employ. They are rare and in much demand. How many are working on the Pit?"

"We currently have two teams," Elias answered. "But it's slow going. This is meticulous work with no room for error."

"I see," Monty said. "This work has been going on for how long exactly?"

Elias glanced at Roxanne who gave him the subtlest of nods. If I hadn't been trained in picking up on those cues, or had blinked, I would've missed it. Monty shifted slightly next to me, letting me know he caught the unspoken interchange between them.

That did not bode well.

"Not very long," Elias said. "We only recently received full approval to begin the inscribing. They needed clearance from Tartarus."

I shuddered at the name, recalling that Tartarus was a place and a being. One I had the bad luck of facing off against a while back.

"Hades sealed that plane for a reason," Monty said his words clipped. "Tell me no one has attempted to venture there without an army of mages."

Elias shook his head.

"That's the reason the Directors approved the inscribing of the Pit," Elias said. "Tartarus isn't easily accessible any longer. The Pit would start the creation of another maximum security detention center."

"The more I hear about this, the less I like," Monty said, pulling on a sleeve. "Are the Directors certain this is the best course of action?"

"Yes," Roxanne answered. "Though the vote went through despite my dissent. The other Directors feel we need the Pit up and running, sooner rather than later."

I'd rarely seen Monty livid, but I felt I was getting a good glimpse of it now. The muscles of his jaws flexed a few times, and his expression made the arctic winter feel balmy by comparison.

I didn't know if it was the fact that this Pit was being actively worked on without his knowledge, or that Roxanne was having secret communications with Elias. Monty never struck me as the jealous type, but I knew he was fiercely territorial of what he considered his.

And that included Roxanne. The same way he was willing to sacrifice his life for her, if need be.

Monty was going to have to address this, but knowing him the way I did, he would do it after he pulled off his plan regarding his great uncle.

It was not going to go over well.

Roxanne would view Monty's plan as some kind of betrayal, and Monty would bring up the work on the Pit and his being left out of the loop as a response.

It would only get worse from there.

It was time to head this off before it exploded and took us all out. Was I going to make things worse? Probably, but I had a feeling that after Monty did whatever he was going to do, it was going to be disastrous anyway.

Why not jumpstart the apocalypse?

"Roxanne, before Elias opens the door to the Well, were you going to tell Monty about the work on the Pit?" I asked. "Or is this classified need to know Haven work, and only Haven Security personnel and Directors could have access to this closely guarded information?"

I figured that should give her enough of an out.

If she was honest and Monty was open to listening to reason, we could prevent a catastrophe of misunderstandings. If not, well, I figured standing at ground zero between a mage of Monty's strength and a sorceress of Roxanne's power, meant the end would be quick.

"You do realize I'm not the only Director at Haven," she said, glancing at Monty before turning to me. "The Pit and all of the work done on it is out of my purview."

"I know there are other Directors," I said. "There's no way you want to handle all of Haven on your own."

"Not in the least, besides, my responsibility lies in the Medical Wing and certain sections of the Detention Wing, like the Well. The Pit is off-limits."

"Then why did they inform you of what was going on there?"

"I was only informed because of my position as a Director. Even I don't know the extent of the work being done on it, nor does Elias or any of my team. Everything concerning the Pit falls under the Maximum Security Protocol and is being handled by the same group that oversees Tartarus."

"Tartarsauce the place, not the angry being, right?" I asked. "Hades sealed the plane, but it's still being used as a prison?"

"The most maximum of all prisons, yes," she said. "The Pit will be a close second once it's completed."

"I see," Monty said. "I want to be present when it goes fully operational. That is *not* a request."

Elias nodded.

"Of course, Tristan," Roxanne said. "You should have the necessary clearance considering your recent dealings with the Keepers."

Monty nodded and appeared satisfied.

It was this shift in demeanor that scared me regarding Monty. I knew he was still planning something shady with Salius, and that Roxanne would view it as a betrayal.

It didn't matter to his mage mind. The ends justified the means when it came to situations like this. It was that cold, calculating mind that made mages so dangerous when they went dark.

They could erase you and easily shrug, informing you not to be upset, as they shared that it 'wasn't personal, just business' and go on with their day.

Thankfully Monty had stepped back from that edge, but he remained too close for comfort. Elias and Roxanne stepped to the door and deactivated the runes as they touched various symbols in sequence.

"Two-factor deactivation?" Monty asked. "Clever and secure."

"You need one Director and the Head of Security acting in tandem to unlock this door," Elias said. "The sequence rotates randomly every twenty minutes with the first rune being the clue to the new rotation."

I looked at the number of symbols on the door and shook my head. It had to be impossible to memorize so many different combinations.

"How?" I asked. "You can't possibly know every possible combination."

"The first rune in each sequence is the key and there are a limited number of those," Elias said. "We made plenty of errors in the first few days until we understood that it's based on extrapolating the runic symbols into numbers and following a Fibonacci sequence."

"The key is knowing which number symbolizes which rune," Monty said. "Ingenious. I'm sure *that* information is kept secret."

Elias nodded.

"Directors and high-level security personnel only," he said. "All of the Directors know the key—and myself and other high-ranking Haven Security. The pool is small."

It wasn't small enough.

I glanced at Monty and gave him my 'this is a bad idea' look. All it took was one of these Directors or high-level security to be compromised and this whole setup was blown apart.

Everything about this concerned me, especially if Monty was still planning a Wellbreak with his great-uncle. The door swung open, and we stepped into a long corridor.

It was a duplicate of the corridor we had just been in, covered with dangerous-looking and lethal-feeling runes.

"This isn't overkill?" I asked. "I thought the Well wasn't a cell?"

"It's not," Elias said. "But Sal...well it's not safe for him to be out of his space. This is more for us, than it is for him."

"You're making him sound like some evil darkmage," I said as we moved down the corridor. "Is that who we're visiting?"

"No," Roxanne answered as we came to another simpler door. "He's dangerous, but he's not an overt danger. As long as he remains in the Well, he will be fine and so will this plane."

I glanced at Monty and really hoped he knew what he was doing. If we unleashed a Bestiarist and he suddenly started creating a zoo of supernatural creatures, this whole plan was going to explode in our faces, starting with Roxanne exploding in Monty's direction.

Roxanne knocked on the door.

"Salius," she said, "we have some guests here to see you."

"Splendid," said a voice from the other side of the door. "Please, do come in."

TWELVE

We stepped into a palatial living space.

It was a home that could have fit in any duplex penthouse on Park or Madison Avenue. The first thing that caught my attention was the size.

The place was immense.

"This place is huge," I said as I looked around. "Why is it so large? Do you need a bicycle to go from room to room?"

"To give me the illusion of the outdoors," a voice said from behind one of the many half walls that divided the open plan space. "To make me feel comfortable about never leaving."

I turned to see an older and more dignified version of Monty standing in the living room area of the loft space. If Elias was the opposite of what a sorcerer should look like, Salius was exactly what I expected a mage to look like.

He was tall and wiry, his gray hair was cut short but he wore a substantial goatee. His eyes practically glowed with energy as he invited us into his home.

"Come in, come in," he said, waving an arm at us. "You are all welcome. Hello, Director, Elias. I trust you are both well?"

"We are," Roxanne said, stepping farther into the space. "How have you been?"

"As well as can be expected," he said with a small smile. "It's not everyday I have guests. Who has honored me with a visit?"

Roxanne and Elias stepped to one side so Salius could get a better look at Monty and me. He stepped to the side and looked around Elias and Roxanne. His focus was immediately on…Peaches.

"Is that a hellhound?" Salius asked almost breathless as he stood absolutely still. "You brought me a real hellhound?"

"He does have a bondmate," Roxanne said, pointing in our general direction. "And he's not here for you, he's part of a package."

"A bondmate?" he asked and then his gaze fell on Monty. "Tristan? Is that you? It's been too long, my child. Are you bonded to a hellhound? What brings you to my humble home?"

Salius approached Monty and hugged him, which I knew for a fact was making Monty all kinds of uncomfortable.

It was excellent.

Monty shook his head and managed to gently escape his great-uncle's clutches.

I looked around again, still impressed by the home.

There were even windows, though I knew there had to be magic at work, since windows this far underground were pointless.

These windows showed me a sunny view of a Park Avenue address located near 86th Street. It was so realistic that if I hadn't known I was underground, it would've fooled me.

I stepped over to one of the windows.

We were approximately on the third floor. I noticed the pedestrians and car traffic. The sounds really sold the illusion.

If I closed my eyes, I could be standing on Park Avenue in the middle of the day.

"Impressive, isn't it?" Salius asked. "I'm still torn as to whether I should consider it cruel or clever."

"Why would it be cruel?" I asked. "Aren't these windows here to create a feeling of openness?"

"No matter how gilded a cage is, it is still a cage," Salius said. "I think they are equal parts clever and cruel."

He was dressed casually in a dark blue linen dress shirt with cream linen slacks. His feet were bare and he seemed entirely comfortable and at ease. There were major similarities to Dexter, even more than to Monty, but there was no way they could deny being related.

"This is Simon," Monty said, pointing at me. "He is the hellhound's bondmate."

"*He* is?" Salius said, giving me a once-over, narrowing his eyes at me and then at Peaches. "How? He's no mage. He has some ability, but hardly enough to bond to a hellhound, much less a direct scion of Cerberus."

"As improbable as it seems, they are bonded," Monty said. "See for yourself."

Salius narrowed his eyes at me again. He let his gaze linger over me a little longer; he muttered some things to himself. After a few more seconds, he shook his head.

"You do indeed speak truth, my child," Salius said. "They *are* bonded. A powerful bond indeed." He pointed a finger as he kept scrutinizing me and my hellhound. "How did *you* manage to acquire a hellhound? They are incredibly rare. It is my understanding that Cerberus destroys all of the hellhounds he sires. Is this true? Do you know? Have you seen other hellhounds?"

"He is the only other hellhound I have ever seen," I said, surprised that I didn't pick up on any dangerous or crazy vibes from the old mage, just the average skepticism most elderly people exhibit when their judgment and experience are being questioned. "I seem to remember Hades mentioning something about Cerberus seeing every other hellhound as a threat, though."

"Ah, so it is true!" Salius said, clapping his hands together a few times and pointing at me again, excited to confirm the rumor he suspected. "Did Hades give him to you or did you abscond with him on your own?"

"You want to know if I stole him from Hades?" I asked incredulously. "Seriously?"

"Stranger things have happened," Salius said, lowering his voice conspiratorially and leaning forward. "Did you steal him? Did Tristan help?"

"No, we didn't steal him," I said much to his apparent disappointment. "Hades gave him to me."

"That's not as exciting as you stealing him from Hades in some daring rescue from destruction at the jaws of his sire," Salius said, glancing at Peaches again. "Hades voluntarily gave him to you?"

"Yes," I said. "He didn't want him to be destroyed and suggested I bond with him."

"What a peculiar name though. Peaches?" he said, rubbing his chin as he glanced down at my hellhound. "Why did you name him Peaches? Does this have a specific significance? What kind of name is that for a hellhound? How is Peaches supposed to strike fear in your enemies. That name just makes me want to give him a hug and maybe a treat or two."

Peaches's ears perked up at the word, 'treat'.

<*He has treats? You heard him, my name makes him want to give me a treat. Tell him my name again, he may have meat here waiting to be eaten. I can help him.*>

<*How can you possibly be hungry? You just got a treat a little while ago. Wasn't that enough?*>

<*Enough? Enough for what? There is no such thing as enough*

meat. As my bondmate, you should know this. I thought everyone knew this? There is never enough meat.>

"The name came with the hellhound," I said. "But it's perfect for him."

"May I...may I pet him?" Salius asked tentatively. "It's been a very long time since I have had any type of animal company. I would consider it a great favor if you do me the honor."

"Salius," Roxanne said, a warning in her voice. "He cannot be altered or controlled. He is bonded. Please refrain from trying to do so."

"I thought there was no casting down here?" I asked Monty under my breath. "Why is she warning him?"

"Because his discipline is little understood," Monty answered in the same tone. "They have placed neutralizing runes throughout his flat, but he has managed to circumnavigate them in the past."

I nodded at Salius and he approached Peaches slowly, extending a hand and rubbing my hellhound's massive head. Peaches sat absolutely still and enjoyed every moment of the rub, the ham.

"I would never attempt such a thing on a bondmate," Salius said, feigning offense as he continued rubbing my obviously deprived hellhound, who leaned into the rub, going so far as to even take a few steps closer to Salius, to provide more access to the area behind his ears. "Aside from the impossibility of such an act on a bonded creature, what do you take me for?"

"A wily mage who would use or create any opportunity to go have a stroll outside. What was it you called it the last time you managed to liberate yourself from the restraints of Haven?"

"I have no idea what you're talking about."

"Oh, yes," Roxanne continued as the memory came back

to her. "You were going to 'shake off the shackles of Haven' and embrace the great outdoors. Then you proceeded to create a herd of pegasi."

"They were glorious," Salius said wistfully. He turned to Monty and me. "You should have seen them, powerful and majestic. They almost got away too." He glanced at Elias. "Except that was prevented."

"Why don't you tell them *why*?" Roxanne said. "Tell them why they had to be apprehended? Aside from the fact that pegasi flying around the city would be generally frowned upon by all of the authorities in this city."

"Because you have lost the wonder of your youth?" Salius said. "Perhaps you have forgotten how to embrace the joy in your life? You really should get out more, away from the stodgy offices of Haven."

"In that glorious, majestic, and powerful herd of pegasi, what Salius fails to mention is that he had created several Dark Pegasi."

"It wasn't intentional, but it is the order of things," he said. "Where there is light, there will be darkness. Where there is order, there must be chaos."

His last words chilled me to the bone.

Anytime Chaos came up in my life, it reminded me that he was out there somewhere...waiting to end Monty and me. I knew that one day we would have to face and end him somehow, I just didn't know if that was even possible.

He was one of the old gods. Probably one of the oldest.

I shook off the chill and refocused on Roxanne who was explaining what the renegade Dark Pegasi were doing.

"They were attacking people," Roxanne continued. "People who had no way of understanding what a pegasus was, except for what they learned in movies and stories. The cleanup from that incident alone was staggering."

"It was so bad it even created the Pegasus Protocol for

security training," Elias said. "It became required study for all current and new security personnel."

"I'm pleased I could be of service," Salius said with a smile and a slight bow. "It's the least I could do."

"I'd prefer it if you did even less," Roxanne said. "Tristan, what did you want to ask him? We've already been down here too long."

It was time for Monty's plan.

THIRTEEN

"Great Uncle Salius—?"

Salius raised a hand and shook his head.

"We'll have none of that," he said. "I understand we're family but, let's not rest on formalities. Call me Sal, please, afford an old man a small comfort."

Monty raised an eyebrow and brushed off his sleeve as he reset his question. I could tell he was uncomfortable with the lack of formality.

It probably went against his way of being as a mage. He was used to rules and regulations. That included following the formal manners of address for his elders or those in positions of power.

That probably didn't apply to Dexter though, and Salius was closer to Dexter in his behavior than any of the other Montagues I had encountered.

"Very well, Sal," Monty said. "What can you tell me about Demogres?"

"Demogres, you say?" Salius said tapping his chin. "Fierce, mobile mage destroyers. They possess nullification fields, which make casting impossible as a counter. The best way to stop one would be to employ close quarter weapons."

"Like a sword?" I asked. "Would those work?"

"Yes and no," Sal said. "They need to be specifically runed as seraph weapons due to the Demogre being partly demonic. An ordinary sword would only serve to end your life in a short and gruesome death."

"A seraphic weapon can stop a Demogre?"

"Yes," Sal said. "But you still have to get close. There is an area, right here"—he stepped close to me and tapped a section of my chest near my heart—"where you need to puncture the Demogre with said weapon. That will end its existence."

"How would a Bestiarist, for example one of your caliber, deal with a Demogre?" Monty asked. "Would you need a seraphic sword?"

"Don't be silly, child," Sal said. "I could reduce it to its component parts, removing the demonic from the ogre, rendering it inert and harmless. It's not easy or simple, but any decent Bestiarist can accomplish this task, provided they know how."

Monty glanced at me and I knew he was going to execute his plan.

"Sal," Monty said, "would you like an opportunity to confront a Demogre?"

"That would be quite spectacular," Sal said with a nod as he looked away to the fake windows. "But alas, child there are no such creatures down here. It would be a wonderful opportunity. Did you know Demogres are not evil?"

"They're not?" I asked. "The one we faced seemed pretty bent on erasing us from this life."

"That's just it," Sal said, entering his professor mode. In that moment, I realized every mage had some version of this mode and that once they got started, it was nearly impossible to stop them from oversharing. "During the war, they were employed as weapons, but they weren't truly understood. Demogres are affected by ambient energy. It causes them excruciating pain, so much so that they lash out at the nearest source."

"Mages?" I asked. "Mages hurt them?"

"Precisely!" he said, tapping me on the shoulder. "Somehow, they are keenly attuned to the energy fields mages produce. In their effort to seek relief, their minds create a direct equation. Remove the mage means remove the pain."

"Tristan?" Roxanne asked warily. "What are you doing? You know Sal can't confront a Demogre. He can't leave the Well."

"He can't or he isn't being allowed to leave?" Monty asked. "What if I could assure you he wouldn't unleash a menagerie of creatures on the city?"

"You can't possibly assure something like that," Roxanne said. "We should leave."

"Does this mean I don't get to confront a Demogre?" Sal asked. "I was looking forward to seeing a Demogre. Are you sure I can't step outside for a day or two?"

"Quite sure," Roxanne said and nodded to Elias. "This visit is concluded."

Ortiz, Walters, and Baker fanned out and took defensive positions around the entrance to the Well. I had already moved closer to Monty and Sal, with Peaches standing by my side.

Monty had promised that he wouldn't hurt them, and he was a mage of his word. If he said he wouldn't hurt them, it meant he had another method of escape that didn't require running the gauntlets of death we had used to get down here.

"He's my family," Monty said, his voice dangerous. "You are keeping him down here trapped like some prisoner. Against his will."

"No," Roxanne said, lifting a hand. "That is not what is happening here. You know we would never—"

"Can he leave whenever he wants?"

I noticed Elias shift ever so slowly to stand closer to his team. These were highly trained sorcerers who knew how to work as a unit. Against anyone else, I would have given them the win.

But they were up against *us*.

They may have been a highly trained unit, but so were Monty, Peaches, and me. We had faced every kind of monster, creature, and being, bent on world destruction. We had even stood against gods and dragons.

A four-sorcerer security team wasn't going to make me think twice. That didn't mean I underestimated them. I didn't *want* to attack them. I considered Elias a friend, and I knew there was no way Monty would or could attack Roxanne, but in this battle, there was no question where I stood.

I was his *Aspis* and they knew this.

"You know he can't," Roxanne answered, staring at Monty, her voice becoming just as dangerous. I realized these two were meant for each other. Monty didn't fear Roxanne and she felt no fear of him. "Tristan, you don't want to do this, you *can't* do this. The Well is a self-contained environment. You can't cast down—"

Monty gestured and formed a bright white orb that nearly blinded everyone.

"Bloody hell," Roxanne said. "How did you do that?"

"Sal?" Monty said calmly. "Would you like to go outside?"

"Tristan, no," Roxanne said. "No!"

"Yes," Sal said, fixated on the orb of power Monty held. "Can you take me outside?"

"Yes," Monty said and glanced at Sal. "I need your help

with a Demogre and after that, I have a special place where you can stay and make as many creatures as you want."

"Impossible," Elias said. "Mr. Montague, you're making a grave mistake. Cease and desist, or we will be forced to—"

"Stop this, Tristan," Roxanne said softer this time. "I know he's family, but think about what you are doing. He is a clear and present danger the moment he steps outside of this facility."

"He wasn't meant to stay down here indefinitely," Monty countered. "The Directors deemed it the safest course of action. I'm sure they explained it was a necessary step for the greater good, yes?"

"Yes, it was deemed the best course of action, considering the threat posed," Roxanne answered after a pause. "It's for the best."

"You agreed with this?" Monty asked. "You condoned this?"

"For the safety of my city and this facility, yes."

"I disagree," Monty said. "This isn't personal. The rest of the Directors will be informed as to my actions here today, and you will not be compromised in any way."

"That's wishful thinking," she said. "They know of our involvement. They will immediately implicate me in this act."

"They will not," Monty said. "This is not a Haven matter any longer, this is a family affair from this moment forward."

"Your family?" Roxanne asked. "What are you saying?"

I was thinking the exact thing, what was he saying?

"You'll find the Montagues have a considerable amount of influence, that we rarely choose to wield," Monty replied and absorbed the orb of power. "Sal, are you ready to leave?"

"Absolutely," Sal said. "But they're blocking the only exit."

Roxanne had grown silent, but I could sense her reaching for power. She just couldn't quite reach it, neither could Elias and his team.

Down here, they had to rely on their weapons.

Honestly, I didn't know how Monty was pulling this orb off. He wasn't supposed to be able to cast down here, no one was. The only explanation I could imagine was that he had grown stronger after the whole First Elder and Keeper situation.

Much, much stronger.

"Not the only exit," Monty said. "Just the most obvious. Forgive me, Roxanne, but as the alternative would be to engage you, Elias, and his team in combat. That would be a step too far."

"I'd say you've gone beyond a step too far. You are dooming this city to a nightmare of monstrous creatures if you do this."

"No, I'm not, but I don't expect you to understand that right now," he said as a large green circle formed under us. "Occasionally, we must take steps that are misunderstood."

"This is about the Pit, isn't it?"

"No, it's not," he said. "But I would be dishonest if I said I agreed with the Board of Directors. However, that is a discussion for another day."

"They won't change their minds," she said. "The Pit will be operational sooner rather than later."

"That remains to be seen," Monty said. "I'm certain the Board and I can have a conversation where I can illuminate them on the hazards of opening the Pit too soon. You should have told me."

"Occasionally, we must take steps that are misunderstood."

The edge of the circle crackled with energy, forcing everyone back several feet. I realized that if any of the sorcerers outside the circle attempted to get in, they would quickly reconsider some of their life choices as massive amounts of pain greeted them on the attempt.

I understood that somehow, Dexter was involved in this. He was the one the reason why managed was able to cast in the Well.

If I thought Dexter was scary before, this new, perceived fear factor had just ratcheted up several levels. Even I had to step away from the edge of the circle, and I was inside of it.

"A safeguarded circle," Roxanne said, looking down at the circle. "You involved Dexter in this?"

"You have it wrong," Monty said, shaking his head. "He involved me."

"I will find you, Tristan," she said calmly, which was worse than if she had screamed those words. "You can't hide."

"I'm not hiding," Monty replied just as calmly. "I do, however, need my great-uncle to deal with this Demogre. That was not a fabrication."

"No, just a convenient excuse," she said. "How long have you planned this? Do you really think you can escape? Didn't you see the runes in place?"

"I already have," Monty said. "It's only a matter of time."

"On your word as bond, you will give me a full explanation of these events," Roxanne said. "Every detail."

"On my word as bond," he said. "Everything will be explained."

Roxanne nodded as she seethed and the waves of controlled rage came off her. Her angry expression was the last thing I saw as I felt the surge of energy that rushed into the circle.

A blast of bright green energy exploded around us, and the Well disappeared.

FOURTEEN

We reappeared in the back room of the Randy Rump.

"You are so dead," I said when we arrived. "She is going to kill you. No, erase that. She is going to kill you, use some sorcerous dark magic, bring you back, and then kill you again."

"We'll deal with that later," Monty said, moving over to a large circle on the floor I didn't remember being there in the past. "Right now, we worry less about Roxanne and more about Esti and Dira, who *definitely* want to kill you."

"When was that inscribed?"

"Not too long ago," Monty said. "My uncle felt it was important to establish a network of teleportation circles for situations such as this."

I held up a hand.

"When?"

"You'll need to be a bit more specific," he said as he entered the circle and started touching symbols. "My powers of telepathy are somewhat rusty."

"When did you get this all set up?" I asked, confused. "Salius, this circle, and how did you even cast in the Well?"

"I was being forthright with Roxanne when she mentioned my uncle Dexter," he said, not looking up from the symbols as he activated them. "I didn't bring *him* into this, he brought *me* into it. He had been planning on retrieving Salius for some time now after discovering that he wasn't being allowed to leave the Well."

"That was wrong," I said, glancing over at Salius, who was examining some of the runes on the large Buloke door. "Was Roxanne part of that? I can't believe she was part of that."

"She wasn't, but she *should* have told me what was happening."

"She probably didn't because she knew you were going to do something like this," I said, "and she wanted to prevent the blowback from you going ballistic."

"I didn't go ballistic," he said. "I was the opposite of ballistic. I remained calm, cool and collected."

"If you say so," I said not believing a word. "The temperature dropped to subarctic when she gave Elias the subtle nod."

"I didn't appreciate the subterfuge," he said. "We will need to discuss that in the future."

"Well you did keep your cool," I said. "There was a time when you may have blasted Elias into outer space for participating in that little communication."

"Why? I'm not in a relationship with him," Monty said giving me a glance. "If I need to have a conversation with anyone it would be with Roxanne. The same way if you had an issue with your vampire, you would speak with her, not those who are tangential to your relationship."

"So you weren't jealous?"

He looked up at me and stared for a few seconds.

"I understand, you're still young," he said. "At my age, I don't do jealousy. What I am is fiercely territorial. Roxanne is mine, the same way I am hers. There's no room for anyone else in my life or heart...for either of us. We established this long ago. That aspect of us is never in question. Are you jealous of your vampire?"

"Why would I be jealous of Chi?"

"Well, if you think about it, there must have been plenty of offers to be her consort," he said as he got back to the symbols in the circle. "She is powerful and the Dark Council vampires must be numerous. Power attracts men...and women."

"You know we've never really discussed it," I said. "We're bonded. She knows how I feel and I know how she feels. There's also that little matter of my not aging. I don't know how I feel being involved with anyone knowing one day they would grow old and die."

"Well, you picked appropriately in this case," he said. "For all intents and purposes, as long as she doesn't take up sunbathing, and keeps herself blooded, real or synthetic, she will be around as long as you are. That must be a warm thought."

I thought I saw the hint of a smile but he kept his face down as he activated and shifted the symbols around in the circle.

"Sure, we'll go with that as a warm thought," I said, shaking my head. "How did you arrange the logistics of the planning though?"

"I didn't, I merely did as instructed. Now my Uncle Dexter? When he heard what the Board of Directors had agreed on, *he* went ballistic. The Directors at Haven escaped from this situation relatively unscathed, for now."

"I don't follow," I said. "What do you mean relatively unscathed?"

"Which is worse? Having me show up and remove Salius with this?" He removed a transparent ring that gave off a subtle green glow from a finger and placed it on the floor outside of the circle. "Or have the Harbinger of Death show up with Nemain at Haven to have a brief conversation on shortened life expectancies with the Board of Directors regarding their policy of holding mages they deem dangerous in a detention center? Against their will, I might add."

"Oh," I said with a slight shudder, thinking about Nemain. "That would be all kinds of bad. Fine, that sort of explains the whole Salius thing. How did you cast in the Well?"

He pointed to the ring he had just placed on the floor and, I approached to get a better look at it.

"That ring is a runic storage device," he said, glancing at the ring that still glowed. "We used them during the war to conserve energy or to mask our signatures, while we entered certain enemy territories. They can store a limited amount of energy and are perfect for casting where you aren't supposed to—like null zones."

"Can I?" I asked, reaching for the ring. "Is it safe?"

"Yes, it's been completely drained," he said still touching symbols. "That is what allowed me to cast the orb. The teleportation circle was a specially designed cast created by my uncle. It's called a retriever and keyed to the mobile repository."

"The what?"

"The ring."

"Ah, got it," I said, picking up the ring and examining it. As I held it, power thrummed through its surface. I could see the runes inscribed on the inside, which reminded me of another ring of power. "How many of these repositories are there? Or is this the only one?"

"Don't," Monty said, without looking at me. "I know where you're going and no, it is not the one ring to rule anything. Stop, while you're behind."

"Fine, suit yourself, I was just asking an innocent question."

"No such thing with you."

"Well, what about the whole Demogre set up? That was just too convenient."

"You recall your vampire was at the School for Battle Magic while we visited?"

"Yes," I said. "That was when she showed me she could still kick my ass and told me about her plans to step down as Director of the Dark Council, so she can deal with the threats to the city."

"Those threats being specifically the Blood Hunters, and Esti, along with the Heretics of the Sanguinary Order," he said, getting to his feet. "She had discovered Esti had access to a Demogre and shared that with my uncle Dexter. He knew it was only a matter of time before Esti unleashed it on us."

"Us? You mean *me*," I said. "She unleashed it on me."

"No," he said, shaking his head. "The Demogre is a greater threat to a mage than to you. She had no way of knowing if it would nullify your curse."

"She's hedging her bets," I said. "Get rid of you, fill me with a few arrows, and then what, come remove my head?"

"She wouldn't do that herself," he said. "She needs to test you first. Use a weapon purported to have god-killing properties."

"That's what Dira and Chandra are for," I said. "The Demogre was to keep you busy while she filled me with arrows and then Dira would arrive and dispatch me?"

"Or something similar," he said. "The Demogre was to run interference on me. It would keep me at bay, or kill me, while she executed her plan to remove you…permanently."

"So Dex was playing super 4D chess waiting on the Demogre to appear to use it as a pretext to collect Salius?"

"Salius is a Bestiarist, who as far as I'm aware can neutralize it, but we're not putting him in harm's way," Monty said. "I'd say he's earned some time to enjoy his freedom, don't you think?"

"Way past time," I said. "But then who is going to neutralize the Demogre? Do we have a backup Beastie Boy?"

"Bestiarist," he said with a sigh. "Not Beastie Boy. Why do I entertain your mangling of names?"

"Because my names are ten times better, admit it."

"I admit nothing and no, we do not have a backup Bestiarist."

"Then who's going to face the Demogre?"

"We are," Monty said. "Salius can walk me through the neutralization cast."

I glanced at Salius, who was still examining the runes in the door. I noticed that my hellhound had approached Salius and watched him read the runes. Salius must have had a natural affinity for supernatural creatures.

"I don't know if anyone has told you, but you're not a Beastie Boy."

"No, I've never been, and never will be a Bestiarist," he said. "But I can simulate the neutralization cast, if Salius teaches it to me, and don't forget we both possess seraphic blades."

"Dex is thinking dozens of steps ahead," I said "That's layers on layers of scary forethought. Does he have a plan for dealing with Esti and Dira?"

"Yes, it's called the Montague and Strong Detective Agency," Monty said. "He has other situations he's dealing with concurrently, like the Pit for instance.

"The Pit? Why is that an issue? Sounds like a good idea to have an alternate place to put supernatural criminals."

"Yes, because that always works out so well," he said. "Confine a being full of primordial power, give said being time to plan and work his or her machinations, and pretend that the safeguards you have in place will work indefinitely and that they have no vulnerabilities. Capital concept, what could possibly go wrong?"

"When you put it that way, it sounds like a horrible idea."

"Because it is," he said. "I knew about the activation of the Pit before Roxanne decided it was time to share."

"Dexter?"

He nodded.

"He really is going to have a conversation with the Board about creating another Tartarus," he said. "It's too dangerous right now, but they don't see that. They want the prestige of having a Maximum Security Detention Center located under Haven."

"How is that prestigious?"

"In the magical community being able to boast of having a facility that can hold the powerful is a matter of prestige." he said. "If a certain creature or being is powerful and yet we can hold them, that makes us even more powerful, or so the flawed logic goes."

"Until the being breaks out, like Tartarsauce did, and proceeds to kidnap Persephone," I said. "Hades was not pleased."

"That is the inherent danger in creating places like that," he said. "They are never perfect, and always have some flaw, which reveals itself over time."

"Hades had to seal Tartarus in the place in order to deal with him," I said, recalling the time we faced Tartarus the being. "Don't they know what happened? It took a god…a *god*, to seal Tartarsauce away."

Monty shook his head and walked over to the table as I handed him the ring.

"Power is a heady thing," he said, placing the ring in a pocket. "No one is really immune to its allure."

"Truth," I said, looking over to where Salius was still examining the door's runes. "What are we going to do with Salius now? He can't stay in here forever. Elias will find him eventually, and they will take him back to the Well."

"He's not going to the Well, ever again," Monty said, his voice hard, before he turned to his great-uncle. "Salius? Would you like to live somewhere where you can create freely without worrying about your creations becoming threats?"

Salius turned to Monty with a sad but hopeful look on his face.

"No such place exists, child," he said. "If it did, I would be there."

"It didn't when you voluntarily surrendered to Haven," Monty said. "However, it does now. Would you like to go there?"

Salius nodded.

"Very much so."

"We are going there shortly," Monty said. "I'm just waiting for James to make some additional preparations."

Jimmy walked into the back room.

"The jump-off point is ready," Jimmy said as he closed the massive door behind him. He walked up to me and rubbed Peaches's head a few times. He reached into his apron and fed him a large sausage. My hellhound inhaled the meat in a millisecond and rumbled his pleasure at Jimmy. "Strong, I know you can't stay, but I packed you a doggie bag for the best hellhound ever."

He handed me a bag that easily weighed ten pounds.

"This is a doggie bag?" I asked. "What is this, the industrial size?"

"He's an industrial-sized hellhound," Jimmy said, before turning to Monty. "You better get going. Dex said you have to keep moving."

I shook my head.

"He's a werebear," Sal said, sounding surprised as he pointed at Jimmy. "They are fascinating members of the were-creature family. Much stronger than wolves and deadlier as well."

"Thanks?" Jimmy said. "Pleasure to meet you as well."

"James, please forgive him," Monty said, motioning to Salius. "This is my great-uncle, Salius, he possesses a particular interest in beings of all sorts."

"I noticed," Jimmy said. "Since you're family, you're welcome to come by any time and we can have a conversation about werebears."

"I would truly appreciate that," Salius said looking at Monty, then back to Jimmy. "Very little is known about werebears. Do we have some time—I would love to conduct an interview regarding the transformational process of human to Ursidae."

"Another day," Monty said. "We do have to get moving and we are somewhat pressed for time."

"We are?" I asked. "Since when?"

"Since your signature is acting like some sort of beacon for Dira and Esti," he said. "We have one quick stop to make, drop off Salius, and then we go to war."

He stepped into the circle and motioned for us to join him.

Salius and I joined him in the circle, and Jimmy and the Randy Rump vanished in a flash.

FIFTEEN

The circle led us to the Montague School of Battle Magic.

We stood in an area I wasn't familiar with. It looked like a large park but this was different from the Morrigan's Grove which felt like an extension of her energy.

This place felt raw as if it were still in the creation stage.

"What is this place?"

"The Menagerie," the Morrigan said from behind us, startling me in the process. "Welcome."

"Are you deliberately trying to give me a heart attack?" I asked, turning on her. "Why do you sneak up on us?"

"I'm not *sneaking* anywhere," she said with a small smile. "Do you really think I have the need or inclination to skulk about?"

"Then what do you call it?" I asked. "One moment you're not there and the next you are. That seems pretty skulky to me."

"I am preparing you," she said. "To date, you are still quite unprepared."

"Preparing me? How is popping up on me unannounced preparing me for anything?"

"You're not paying attention—in more ways than one," she said. "If I'm not hiding, what does that mean?"

The realization hit me then.

If she wasn't sneaking about, it meant that I wasn't sensing her energy signature. Was she doing this only to me? Or was she doing this across the board for everyone in the School?

I wanted to know.

"Did you sense her approach?" I asked, turning to Monty. "You sensed her before we heard her voice?"

"I don't think using my ability to sense her would be an accurate measurement of your abilities or a clear indicator of how honed your senses currently are," he said. "You have to understand, I've had many more years of training."

"Cut the crap, Monty," I said, seeing through the smokescreen. "You can just say you sensed her before we heard her."

"Don't feel bad," he said. "She's a goddess, not exactly an easy task. This is actually good training. Once you can sense her, I doubt anyone will be able to approach you without your knowing."

"I have no idea how this is even training," I said. "A clue would be good."

"I know just the person you need to speak to," he said and turned to the Morrigan. "Well met, Morrigan. Is my uncle available?"

"I'm afraid not," she said. "He has tasked me with relocating your great-uncle, Salius, I presume?"

"Morrigan?" Salius said. "As in *the* Morrigan? The Chooser of the Slain? That Morrigan?"

"The one and the same," Morrigan said with a slight head nod. "I'm here to show you to your new home."

"Have I died?" Salius asked, looking around. "Or about to?"

"Neither," Morrigan said. "Consider this place your new

retirement home where you can create to your heart's content."

"Truly?" Salius asked. "I can create anything?"

"With one caveat," she said. "If anything you create destroys any of the grounds or property, you will be responsible for its repair. If you can adhere to that one condition, then yes, you can create anything."

"Anything?" I asked. "Even creatures like ogres?"

"Even creatures like ogres," she said. "Ogres, dragons, trolls, trollgres, goblins, kobolds, and the like are not inherently evil, just like no spell or rune is inherently evil."

"I've yet to meet an ogre that just wants to talk," I said. "They usually want to have a few words, but those words are almost always: 'die, I'm going to kill you, surrender so I can rip your arms off and beat you to death with them.' It's never been, 'good afternoon, how are you today? Wonderful weather we're having, or pleasure to meet you.'"

"Well, you've been moving in very violent circles as of late," she said with a straight face. "You should consider expanding your circle, getting out more and seeing the world. Not every ogre wants to kill you."

"I'll believe that when I see it," I said. "Are these creatures just going to roam around? What about the eventual students who will be here? Won't they be in danger?"

"Apprentices and beginning students will not be allowed into the Menagerie," she said. "Not until they have mastered the defensive arts and have demonstrated a proficiency in basic Bestiary. Likewise, the potentially dangerous creatures will be confined to the Menagerie, but will be free to roam within its confines."

"And Salius?" I asked. "Is he confined too? Because that would make the whole exercise of breaking him out pointless."

"Salius is free to live in his home, located in the center of the Menagerie, or he can choose to live on campus at the school. He is free to do as he wishes and to go anywhere on this plane."

"Oh, wow," I said, surprised. "That is...well, that is excellent. What do you think Salius?"

Salius had his hands cupped and was whispering something into them. He said a few more things I couldn't quite hear and then opened his hands.

A kaleidoscope of the largest, bluest butterflies erupted from his hands. Each radiated power and glowed brightly in the noonday sun.

They burst upward, fluttered around Salius a few times and took off deeper into the Menagerie. I stood there transfixed as the blue cloud of insects fluttered away.

"I think I'm going to enjoy it here," Salius said, looking at the Morrigan. "Thank you. Thank you so much, all of you."

"You are most welcome," the Morrigan said. "The thanks goes to Dexter—we all played a small part—but this was truly his idea. Tristan, I do believe there's a matter of a Demogre to discuss?"

"Yes," Monty said with a short nod. "Could you direct us to Salius's new home?"

"Follow the path," Morrigan said, pointing at the deep red stones in front of us. "It will lead you directly to his home. Dexter wished to express his gratitude at you accepting his invitation by offering you this humble gift as a token. I hope you enjoy it."

"I have no way to repay what he has given me up to this moment," Salius said as he choked up. He took a moment to compose himself and nodded. "He has my sincerest gratitude in return. He has given an old man wings."

The Morrigan smiled and it was a real smile, not one designed to drive a stake of fear into your heart and turn your blood to ice.

"Very well," she said, "I have other matters to attend to and two young ladies bent on wreaking havoc to assign tasks to. I will visit at a later date, and Dexter will come see you when he returns."

Salius nodded and then bowed.

"My deepest thanks," he said. "I'm looking forward to seeing Dexter again. It has been too long."

"Indeed," she said. "Until then."

She took several steps and then vanished.

I stood absolutely still and focused, letting my senses expand. After a few moments, I barely sensed her energy signature behind me.

Then she was gone.

SIXTEEN

It turned out that Dexter's humble token of gratitude was an enormous mansion with acres of land around it.

"That's some gift," I said. "Dex knows how to splurge."

"That he does," Monty said, standing next to me and looking at the property. "This is quite impressive."

"This is my house?" Salius said. "What am I going to do with all that space?"

"A good question," Monty said. "One you don't need to answer right away. I will, however, offer you some direction. Have you ever considered teaching those interested in the Bestiary Arts?"

"You mean teach other Bestiarists?

"Yes, it's a rare discipline, and it doesn't have to die out," Monty said. "Here, you can help train a new generation of Bestiarists."

"I would need my texts and a lab," Salius said, slowly getting excited at the prospect of being able to teach students about his discipline. "I've always wanted to share what I know, but it was always frowned upon at the sect."

"I can imagine, even mages fear what they don't understand—especially mages, actually," Monty said. "We prefer to have the how and why of things before accepting them."

"Too true," Salius said. "Let's discuss the neutralization cast."

"Here?" Monty said. "You don't want to see the inside of your home first?"

"I have the rest of my life to do that," Salius said. "Right now, I need to prepare you to meet and defeat a Demogre."

"Not kill?" I asked. "I mean I'm noticing you didn't say kill or exterminate, eradicate or disintegrate the Demogre, just defeat. That means we are to keep it alive."

"Yes," Salius said, gesturing, and with a flick of his wrist, a dozen of the deepest, red-colored hummingbirds I had ever seen, materialized in front of us. "Do you know what these are?"

"Troch Liday's Vengeance," Monty said, his voice low. "She was a Master Bestiarist who was persecuted, tortured, and killed for her abilities."

"Yes," Salius said, extending a hand as several of the beautiful birds perched on his shoulders, arms and hand. "She *was* killed, but not before she created these beautiful creatures and shared the method with every Bestiarist of her time with one instruction."

"Every Bestiarist must learn Troch Liday's Vengeance, that they may never be defenseless as I once was," Monty said. "Every mage knows her story. During the war, we called them the Bloody Death."

"Do you know why they were called this?" Salius asked, reaching for my arm and holding it up as one of the hummingbirds perched on my hand. There were a few standing on Peaches, who sat calmly as if the birds weren't even there. "Liday made something truly unique and spectacular in these birds."

"They weren't weapons, they formed defensive perimeters

that were impenetrable," Monty said. "offering mages cover when under attack. Their bodies are nearly indestructible—they're mostly immune to magic, requiring a significant blast of power to destroy, and they have one fearsome ability."

Salius touched the hummingbird on my hand and it vanished. I turned my hand and realized that it hadn't vanished but had done a chameleon camouflage maneuver, shifting the color of its feathers to match the color of my hand.

"Why were they called Bloody Death if they were for defensive perimeters?" I asked, turning my hand to look at the bird from different angles. Every time I moved my hand, it adjusted the camouflage to match my angle of perspective. "That's amazing camo."

"Their beaks are stronger than steel," Monty continued. "If they feel you are going to be attacked, their last defensive move is to sacrifice themselves by attacking repeatedly with their beaks. Many mages on both sides lost their lives to the Bloody Death in the war."

"Now," Salius said, turning to me. "knowing the history of this magnificent creature, should I destroy it?"

"It's not trying to kill you," I said, keeping a wary eye on the one perched on my finger just in case Salius decided to activate it to terminate me or something. "There's no reason to kill it."

"And if it were set to kill me?" Salius asked. "Should I kill it then?"

"If a creature is coming to kill me or those I care for, I'm going to stop it," I said. "If that means I have to end its life to keep mine, then that is the choice I will make."

He looked at me for a few seconds and then nodded.

"I respect your principles, as I hope, you respect mine," he said. "Thank you for not reflexively defaulting to killing the creature, but rather intending to stop it first."

"I try not to default to 'everything must die' mode," I said. "Even creatures trying to end my life deserve an opportunity to stop and go back where they came from."

"That's all I ask you offer the Demogre," Salius said. "If you can defeat it and send it here, I can attempt to rehabilitate it. If it's too far gone, then I *will* dispatch it."

I nodded.

"Even a rabid dog is mercifully put down," I said. "Are you saying you're going to face a Demogre alone?"

"Yes," he said. "I can handle a defeated Demogre, if you use the method I'll show you, Tristan."

"I'm ready," Monty said. "Can you break down the sequence?"

Salius nodded and first traced the runes in the air. Then he demonstrated the hand gestures needed to execute the cast. He did this several times until Monty performed it to Salius's satisfaction.

I sat off to the side with Peaches, feeding him the contents of the industrial-sized doggie bag Jimmy had packed. He inhaled it, then plopped down to watch Monty create symbols and work through the sequences.

I felt the vibration of his body hitting the ground. He got comfortable and focused on Monty.

He was snoring in under a minute.

"You grasped this quickly," Salius said. "You have some experience with difficult casts."

"Yes," Monty said. "As of late, most of the casts I've been learning have been coupled with plenty of difficulty."

Talk about the understatement of the century.

Next, Salius traced a large circle in the ground near the path. He entered the circle and motioned for us to enter with him. Peaches remained just outside the circle, but stayed close to me.

"Your weapons, please," Salius said. "May I see them?"

Monty manifested his crybabies.

They wailed as he reached back behind him and pulled them out of the dimension he kept them in. I always wondered why he didn't internalize them the way I did with Ebonsoul. Was it that he couldn't, or that he chose not to have them inside?

"Monty, why don't you have the crybabies inside the same way I have Ebonsoul?" I asked. "Are you afraid you'll start hearing wailing children in your dreams? I could see how that would be a nightmare."

"Does Ebonsoul speak to you in your dreams?"

"Well, no, it doesn't wait until I'm asleep to speak," I said. "It likes to have those 'come to the dark side conversations' while I'm nice and wide awake."

"Exactly," Monty said. "That's why."

"What? That tells me nothing."

Salius extended his hands and Monty handed him the crybabies. They wailed as Salius moved them through the air.

"These are perfectly balanced," Salius said, holding them close to his eyes and examining the runework inscribed on the blades. "This is exquisite craftsmanship. These would work perfectly on any other demon besides the Demogre."

"What?" Monty said. "Besides the Demogre? These are seraphs, that's what they're created for, how could they not be effective against the Demogre?"

"They are superb weapons for dealing with demons," Salius said, holding up a hand to calm the agitated Monty. "A Demogre is a hybrid creature. A demon merged with an ogre. It's neither one nor the other, but a combination of the two." He turned to me. "May I see your blade?"

I formed Ebonsoul, and the edge of the circle erupted in a dark orange flame. Salius raised an eyebrow in a typical Montaguean way and did not extend his hand to take Ebonsoul.

He shook his head when I offered it the way Monty offered his crybabies. I felt slightly offended that he turned down Ebonsoul.

"I don't need to touch it," Salius said. "Please hold it close so I may read the runes."

I did as he asked and refrained from asking why he didn't like Ebonsoul. I took it personally that my blade had been rejected.

"I am not rejecting your blade," Salius said as he glanced at my face. I figured my dejected expression betrayed me. "As you may know, I am a darkmage. Your blade is not only a seraph as Tristan's Sorrows are. This blade you are bonded to holds much death. How can you possibly wield this weapon without experiencing your immediate demise?"

"It's complicated, trust me," I said. "Is that why you won't hold it?"

"No one should be able to hold that blade," he said. "But for a darkmage, it holds an allure. I can feel its pull without holding it in my hands. This blade can confront the Demogre."

"Excuse me?" I asked. "What do you mean this blade can confront the Demogre? That sounds like I'm the one who must get close and fight it."

"Why, yes," he said matter-of-factly. "That's exactly what I mean."

"That sounds hazardous to my long-term health," I said remembering the area-of-effect the Demogre had and how it could nullify my curse. The same curse that prevented me from dying a horrible and gruesome death by being turned to paste by the Demogre. "I've grown attached to some things, like breathing."

"You're not a mage so it won't nullify your magic, and the power inherent in your weapon doesn't emanate from you," Salius said. "You must be the one to strike the blow that will allow for the neutralization cast to take effect. It will need to be a two-pronged attack."

"Simon lowers its defenses by striking the vital point, and then I cast," Monty said. "It can work."

"It's the only way," Salius said. "Tristan, you can't be in range until the vital point is struck" Salius poked a finger in my chest and pressed hard. "You need to hit it right there. It will try to stop you so you will need to be fast and deceptive."

"Oh, really?" I said, totally not enjoying this plan. "It's going to try and prevent me from stabbing it in the vital point that would make it vulnerable, imagine that."

"That's what I said," Salius said. "Weren't you paying attention?"

"I was," I said. "Will this point being struck kill it?"

"No," Salius said. "It will increase in strength, become angered and try to destroy you."

"Of course it will," I said. "Totally didn't see that coming."

"Tristan must have the cast ready. Once executed, you will be able to use your seraph on the demonic portion of the Demogre for a short window of time. Robbed of demonic power, you will be able to subdue it with any number of stasis casts."

"I heard Demogres can cast," I said. "Is that true?"

"Yes, but those are basic casts," he said. "Once you hit that vital point, they will be inconsequential and easily dealt with."

"We can do this," Monty said. "Can we run through the sequence again?"

"Of course," Salius said. "Start from the opening sequence and merge it with an immobilization cast."

Monty ran through the sequence again.

This time, I paid attention.

SEVENTEEN

We left Salius to explore his home as the artificial sun set on the Battle Magic plane.

As we walked back down the path, I realized that there was a real chance I would have to face the Demogre, Esti, and Dira without my immortality to keep me safe.

The thought didn't exactly scare me. It was probably because I hadn't been born immortal. I had been cursed upon me, and some part of my brain was still wondering how true it could be that I was trulyimmortal.

That I couldn't stay dead.

It was far-fetched at the best of times, but now that I might have to face the Demogre without that shield of protection, it sobered my thoughts.

"I may have to face this Demogre without my curse," I said as we walked down the path. "If that area-of-effect negates all magic, there's a good chance I won't be cursed as I face it."

"Are you scared?" Monty asked, after a pause. "You could actually die…permanently."

"Is that your idea of a pep talk?" I asked. "Because honestly, it's more like an anti-morale builder."

"Pep talk? I'm a mage," he said, glancing at me. "If you haven't noticed by now, mages don't do 'pep talks.'"

"Or you're all just horrible at them."

"Simon, morale building is for those who fail to see the reality before them," he said. "I've raced into enemy encampments, faced monsters, confronted gods and goddesses—"

"I get it, I get it," I said, raising a hand. "Mages are fearless, no need to rub it in."

"Actually, no," he said, shaking his head. "I've had to bury most of those who claimed to fear nothing and no one. I would be concerned if you *didn't* feel fear at the prospect of your own mortality."

"*You* were scared?"

"Every single time," he said. "Always remember, fear is a reaction—we all will feel it, but courage is a decision."

"Did you just British Bulldog me?"

"It seemed an apt moment for it," Monty said, with a nod. "We act in spite of fear, because if we don't, who will?"

"We're going to need a plan to corner Dira," I said. "Kali wants me to talk her down and somehow get the sword back."

"You could always ask for it back," Monty suggested. "Perhaps she would listen to reason?"

"She wants me dead," I said. "She feels she deserves to be the Marked One more than I do. How exactly is that request supposed to go? Hey, I know you want to kill me, but that weapon you have, yes, the one that can actually probably kill me, you mind if I get that back? It belongs to another homicidal warrior who won't think twice about removing your head with the very same blade. Thanks."

"Straight and to the point," he said. "You could probably make it more succinct, more along the lines of: 'Hand over the sword Esti gave you and you can live to kill me another day. If you don't, the owner of the sword will end your life.'"

"Definitely punchier," I said. "I don't think she'll listen without force being involved somewhere."

"True, she has proven to be obstinate about the topic of your death being necessary," he said. "You could always unleash your creature on her? He could hold her down while you explain why you taking the sword back is in her best interests."

"I don't think that's going to be so easy."

"By this point, easy should have left your vocabulary," Monty said. "We will need to put you somewhere prominent or, do you happen to have her phone number? That would make this so much easier."

"Oh sure, one second, let me see if I remember it off the top of my head," I said, glaring at him. "How about 1-800-Kill-Simon, Successor Division?"

"Too many digits," Monty said. "We'll have to get her attention using conventional methods."

I stared at him.

Just when I thought he didn't possess a sense of humor, he would say things like that.

"Getting her attention doesn't mean I want to be target practice for Esti and her psychotic arrow brigade," I said. "We need somewhere that would attract Dira, but not give Esti an easy line of sight so she can try to fill me with arrows again."

"Hmm, somewhere accessible but not open," he said. "Exactly how do we get Dira's attention?"

"I think I know a way, but I'm almost positive I'm going to hate it."

"Really? That sounds promising," he said, as we got to the end of the path, which was really the beginning, and approached the campus grounds. "What method?"

"This Chandra blade, Iris has to be bonded to it, right?"

"I assume it would be something similar to what you experience with Ebonsoul," he said. "A deep connection, minus the access to a bloodthirsty goddess. Why?"

"Well, if she's bonded to it, wouldn't she know how to locate it?"

He rubbed his chin and paused as we reached one of the main buildings.

"It's a solid theory," he said. "There's only one snag."

"Getting her to share the location of Chandra without her shredding Dira in the process," I said. "You think she would? Even though Kali told her not to?

"I'm fairly certain Dira could meet with a fatal accident, one facilitated by Iris," he said. "Something like falling and tripping on Chandra, which just happened to be held by Iris at the moment of said *accidental* mishap."

"Kali would be upset, but in the larger scheme of things, the leader of her assassin squad probably outweighs the successor who hasn't managed to retire the current Marked of Kali."

"Kali does seem to operate in an extreme meritocracy."

"Extreme," I said. "That's one way to describe it. You have to prove you're worthy of your title by staying alive."

"Quite the incentive."

"It's insane."

"I'd refrain from sharing that opinion with her in your next chat."

"Wasn't intending to discuss it with her," I said, looking around because you could never be too sure. If I couldn't sense the Morrigan, there was no way I would sense Kali if she didn't want me to. "I'd never suggest that Kali was or is insane."

"Do you have another way to contact Dira that doesn't

involve Iris?" he asked. "Do you happen to have her phone number?"

"What is it with you and phone numbers?" I said, irritated. "No, I don't walk around with phone numbers of actual or potential assassins. Why would you think I did?"

"You have your vampire's number."

"Well, yes, but that's diff—"

He started counting off on his fingers.

"You carry Dex's number. Also, LD's and TK's, you do possess Ezra's number, yes? I'm certain you do."

"You know I do."

"You also know how to contact the Midnight Echelon, since I've been informed you are now considered an honorary member—by the way, congratulations are in order."

"Thanks?"

"Now that I think of it, you recently acquired property in the Underworld and are on a first name basis with the god of the Underworld," he said, tapping his chin. "Few can make that boast."

"That wasn't intentional. Orethe gifted her place to me, and we still don't know the depth of Hades's true agenda. Gods always have hidden agendas."

"Details that don't change the facts, true?"

"True," I admitted. "That doesn't mean—"

"Let's not forget that the blade to which you are bonded, Ebonsoul, was gifted to you by a vampire," he said, cutting me off. "Who, before she was the Director of the Dark Council, spent time as a mythological killer in her home country. She was fearfully known as the Reaping Wind."

"Only in her country."

"Irrelevant," he continued. "Said blade is also very likely a partial receptacle of Izanami, a goddess, who is rumored to be the first true vampire."

"You haven't proven that...yet."

"Nothing a conversation with Grey and his blade can't fix," he said. "Hold on, you also happen to have Grey's number as well, the last Night Warden. A group known to have permanently dispatched a fair number of enemies in the past."

"You made your point."

"Have I?" he asked. "Any of those names I mentioned would qualify as a world-class assassin, and has served as such at some point in their lives, though I don't know if Ezra counts, being Death incarnate. Should I go on?"

"No, thank you," I said, realizing he was right. "I think you're missing the most important factor. There's a *huge* difference between all those you mentioned, and Dira and Esti."

"Oh, pray tell," he said. "Illuminate me."

"Dira and Esti are *actively* trying to kill me," I said, feeling vindicated. "Everyone else you mentioned is not actively trying to end my life."

"Hmm, good point," he said. "I concede you are right. What then is your method for contacting Dira?"

"Kali," I said. "I'm sure she can contact Iris."

"...who should be able to track her sword, which would lead us to Dira," he said. "I like it. Simple and straightforward. Now, you just have to reach out to your goddess."

"She's not my—"

"I also would like to point out that Kali, *your* Kali, also known as Kali the Destroyer, is a goddess of death," he said, rubbing it in. "The trend continues."

"I said, I got it," I snapped. "I'll contact Kali and hopefully she can put me in touch with Iris."

"Are you sure this is safe?"

"You're asking me if contacting a goddess of Death is safe?"

"Yes," he said. "I realize you're her Marked One, but I'm under the impression she is still quite angry with you."

I gave him a three on the glare-o-meter.

"Why don't you pinpoint where we're going to confront Dira?" I asked. "Work out a plan that won't get me killed, and I'll deal with contacting Kali."

"Sounds like an excellent division of labor," he said. "I need to confer with the Morrigan as well. This will kill two birds with one stone."

I raised an eyebrow at his last statement as headed into the main building. I rubbed my massive hellhound's head and let out a long slow breath.

I walked a short distance away from the main building and found a small park. The campus was full of these small areas designed to break up the stone architecture with plenty of green and dotted with benches.

It was a good and peaceful design.

I checked the stone bench before sitting. Knowing Dex, the bench might double as some protective structure, designed to transform into some kind of stone sentry of defense at the first sign of danger.

With Dex you could never be too sure.

My massive hellhound plopped his head on my lap and nearly launched me forward off the bench and onto the ground. I held onto the bench to remain seated.

He immediately doused my pants leg with a broad patch of healing drool. I gently shoved his head off my leg in an effort to save the rest of my pants from being completely saturated with hellhound saliva.

I managed to move his head a few inches and mostly off my leg.

<What's wrong, bondmate?>
<Nothing. Everything.>

<Are you confused? Nothing and everything cannot happen at the same time. If everything is wrong, nothing can't be wrong, and if nothing is wrong, everything can't be wrong.>

I was sitting on a bench in an alternate plane having a deep Zen moment with my Zen Meat Master hellhound. This was surreal.

I shook my head and looked into his deep, softly glowing, red eyes.

<I'm not explaining myself right.>

<Are you hungry? Have you eaten meat lately? Do you still have the meat the Bear man gave you? You can eat some of that.>

<You ate all of that when we were at Salius's house, remember?>

<I forgot that. It was so long ago.>

<We just came from there. It wasn't even an hour ago.>

<Like I said, it was so long ago. Do you know what's wrong now?>

<I have to face a Demogre.>

<We have faced many monsters and creatures, what is one more? We are mighty. We will face this monster, I will face it with you. Wherever you go, I go.>

<This monster is different, stronger than the others.>

<Then we must fight him together in our battle form. We can both bite him.>

<I don't want you biting a Demogre, it's probably bad for you.>

<Are you scared?>

<I won't be protected. I might actually die this time.>

<Why won't you be protected? I will be with you. I will protect you the way you protect me. We are bondmates. If you are hurt, my saliva will heal you.>

I looked into his eyes and realized that I had never explained to him how Kali had cursed me alive. I knew he wasn't a normal or regular dog, but I wondered if he could grasp a concept like immortality.

I rubbed his head again and nodded.

"Time to stop putting this off," I said. "Let's call a goddess."

I pressed my mark.

EIGHTEEN

I still didn't know exactly how my mark worked, but I had a strong feeling intention played a big part of who showed up when I activated it.

I focused on Kali, not Durga.

I didn't need the goddess of creation and light, when Monty and I were going to step into violence and death. I needed to have words with Kali the Destroyer.

I kept my hand on my mark as I focused on my intentions.

Dark blue energy flowed from my mark which was new, as the air around me grew thick with white smoke. Peaches whined next to me, but remained close, as the area around us became obscured by the smoke.

I couldn't see the park or any of the other structures that were around us a few seconds ago. Actually, it felt like we had shifted away from the School of Battle Magic.

I gripped Peaches by the scruff and pulled him closer.

"Stay close, boy," I said, keeping my voice low. "I don't think we're in Kansas anymore."

Peaches gave off a low rumble and stepped into 'protect

and maim' mode. The blue energy stopped flowing after a few seconds. The clouds were thick around us, but I didn't dare move from the bench. It was the only anchor I had to the school campus and I suspected I would get impossibly lost if I stepped away from it.

I felt the energy signature all around me.

Kali wasn't approaching. She was here—everywhere.

I remained still because now I was convinced that rather than calling Kali to me, she had somehow pulled us to her. I shouldn't have been surprised—she was a goddess after all.

Transporting her Marked and his hellhound wouldn't have been difficult. After considering it a little more, this actually made the most sense. Why would a goddess come when I pressed a mark?

Yes, it was *her* mark, but I realized the courtesy she was offering me by showing up when I pressed it. Karma on the other hand was an entirely different story. I think she enjoyed showing up, despite all her protests about it.

I think I made her existence a little less routine and provided some excitement, which she would call stress, but it was definitely not boring.

The clouds began to part as if being blown away, yet I felt no wind. A shadowed figure approached.

Kali.

As she got closer, the clouds parted faster until she was standing a few feet away staring at me. Her blue-black skin glistened with a golden energy that radiated from her.

Her jet-black hair swayed gently behind her as if alive, and her piercing eyes fixed me with a knowing gaze. She sat back and the clouds solidified behind her into a large cushion.

I looked around for her lion, but he must have been busy terrorizing other areas of her home plane. It was also possible that Kali in this form, didn't need to ride a fearsome and powerful lion.

She kind of had the whole fearsome look nailed down all on her own.

She wore a loose white blouse and flowing orange pants. Her feet were bare as usual. What threw me were the additional arms carrying weapons.

Lethal-looking weapons in hands that seemed to move with minds of their own. Two of her arms were crossed over her chest while the other two each held curved blades.

Around her neck she wore a necklace of skulls, and when she licked her lips, her blood red tongue caught my eye.

It was at this moment that I realized I really preferred the Durga version of the Death Goddess. To say I was scared would've been a lie. To say I was scared shitless was closer, but the more accurate description of my current state was, I was terrified out of my mind.

An oppressive aura of terror surrounded us. She sat calmly on her cloud cushion and looked at me, a small smile playing on her lips.

It was all I could do not to run away from her screaming.

"You wanted to speak with me, Marked One?"

I opened my mouth a few times, but nothing came out. I took a deep breath and closed my eyes in an effort to focus. That helped somewhat, but the benefit of that breath disappeared the moment I opened my eyes again.

Was the terror I felt somehow connected to my perception and tied to my vision?

I closed my eyes and the terror intensified.

One theory shut down.

The next moment, the terror completely dissipated from the area. I knew she was still there. The terror was gone, but her overwhelming presence could still be felt.

I peeked my eyes open, and there she sat, not a hallucination of mind-numbing fear.

"Better?" she asked. "You are learning about your intention, but still are not aware of what that entails."

I coughed a few times and found my voice.

"I need to speak to you, this you—not the Durga—nice you."

"You want to speak to this facet of me?" she asked. "Voluntarily?"

"Yes," I said. "I need a favor."

"Immortality was not enough of a favor?"

"You yourself called it a curse," I said, feeling the familiar anger that always rose when I dealt with gods. "Now you're saying my curse is a favor?"

"Always such a stark dichotomy with humans," she said. "Good or evil, curse and favor. Why can't it be both?"

"You're saying my curse is also a favor? I'm not seeing it."

"Yet," she continued. "Consider fire." She formed a large orb of blue-white flame. It was so hot I felt the heat on my face from my bench. "Curse or favor?"

"Depends on how it's used or unleashed."

"Yes," she said and her smile deepened as she gazed on me. "Continue."

"Fire can keep you warm in the cold, and help you cook food," I said, letting the thought run its course. "But it can also burn your house down or burn and kill you. It's both."

"Curse *and* favor," she said with nod. "Another, your immortality. Curse or favor?"

This was a little harder and I should've expected it. On one hand, there were definite pluses to being immortal. Especially when you had the enemies I had. Then I had to consider, if I was mortal would I even have the enemies I had?

Probably not.

This one felt like a snake eating its own tail.

"Harder," I said. "I'm not seeing the downside to living forever and not being able to die."

She steepled two of her hands and placed her index fingers across her lips, resting her elbows on her knees, as her other arms rested beside her, still holding those dangerous looking swords.

I also knew that before I made my request I would have to engage in this verbal sparring. It may have just been words, but I knew deep in my core, this was every bit as dangerous as if I had Ebonsoul in my hand and was standing against the swords in her hands.

"Stretch yourself and try to envision never dying," she said gently. "Close your eyes and let me help you."

I stared at her, not trusting her at all.

"Is that a request?"

"Close your eyes. Now."

"Got it, not a request."

I closed my eyes and stepped into hell.

The first image was an older, much older, Monty. At first I thought it was Dex, but then I recognized him. He's fighting off dozens of ogres and other assorted creatures. For a moment, it looks like he would make it, then he's hit by a blast of black energy.

It causes him to drop his guard. An ogre sees the opening and Monty reacts too slowly in creating a shield.

The ogre's fist makes contact, driving a massive fist into Monty's chest, destroying him and ending his life. He falls back to the ground lifeless, and I'm powerless to do anything.

All I can do is watch.

The image shifts away from Monty to a beautiful sunrise on a beach, which takes me by surprise. I look around, but it doesn't make sense. Why would I be on a beach at sunrise?

"I've always wanted to feel the warmth of the sun on my skin one final time," a voice says next to me. I look to my side and see a smiling Chi staring back as she holds my hand. "Thank you for this, Simon. You will always hold my heart."

"No."

It was all I could manage before the sun crests over the horizon and she's bathed in the brilliant sunlight, blinding me. When I can see again, all I'm holding is dust, which is then scattered away by the wind.

At this point, I didn't want any more of Kali's *help*.

"No more," I said, in an effort to get her to stop. "I think I know the answer, now."

I looked up and around, but nothing.

The image shifted again, the scene I dreaded.

"Stop," I said. "Stop!"

The scene froze.

It was me and Peaches.

We were both bloody and beaten. We were facing a horde of shadowhounds and what looked like all the shamblers ever created, bearing down on us.

It was just us and it didn't look good.

I was covered in gashes and cuts. Peaches had a long cut along one side and it looked like one of his eyes was missing.

I knew this was the end for both of us.

He would never leave my side and I would never leave his. The shadowhounds were close and the shamblers were too many to count.

We were dead, it was only a matter of time.

Kali appeared by my side.

"It looks grim, does it not?"

I locked my jaw and fixed my gaze on the image in front of me.

"It looks like death."

"Yes," she said her expression somber. "In this situation, my curse would keep you alive, but your hellhound would perish. He is not immortal. Nigh indestructible, yes, but even hellhounds have their limits. In addition, to save your life, he would sacrifice his own."

"No."

"Yes," she said with a short nod. "It's what bondmates do."

"I wouldn't let him."

"There would be no choice," she said. "Do you wish to witness his end?"

I turned to her then, my heart and very being full of sadness and something more…fury.

"Why? Why are you doing this?"

"Immortality is both a curse *and* a favor," she said, stretching out an arm to the scene before us. "At present, you only experience the favor, but I *have* cursed you, my Marked One. You won't see it today, or tomorrow, or years hence, but centuries from now, when *all* those you love and cherish are but dust and memories, and you still walk the earth, you will understand the depths of my cruelty."

"You are a bitch," I said and nearly launched myself at her. Only my deep sense of self-preservation prevented me from attacking her. "This is no favor."

She nodded.

"Hold that fury, stoke it," she said as the smile returned. "It will serve you well in the future. Are you certain you do not wish to see the outcome of this battle?"

"I'm certain."

With a wave of a hand, the image vanished.

"Make your request, Marked One," she said. "Now that we have an *understanding*."

NINETEEN

I stomped on my rage and got myself under control.

It would do nothing to lose control. I knew who I was dealing with and Kali wasn't the type of goddess to coddle those she dealt with. I really doubted she cared about her worshippers and I certainly didn't qualify as one.

"You want me to help Dira," I said. "Why?"

"Aside from it being my request?" she asked. "Usually that would be enough."

"Maybe...for those who blindly worship and follow you," I said. "I'm going to need a little more than, you have spoken and let it be so."

Fine, I was definitely running into suicidal territory, but I was beyond angry after that horror fest she had treated me to. I wasn't thinking straight and if I had been thinking at all I would have wanted to face Durga not Kali, but it was too late for that.

"You do realize that immortals can die?" she said matter-of-factly. "Especially when confronted with overwhelming power?"

"If you wanted blind obedience, why curse me?" I asked,

letting the anger write checks my body couldn't cash. "You could have blessed or cursed Dira or any number of followers you have. I'm sure they would have done your every bidding and been willing to lay their lives down for you and your whims."

"But not you?"

"You know for a fact that's not me," I said, getting my anger finally and truly under control. "I serve no god, as far as I'm concerned, all gods have shown me is that absolute power does corrupt absolutely."

"You think me corrupt? Me?"

"Corrupt? No," I said. "Entitled, conniving, devious, deadly, and duplicitous, yes."

"You've just described most of the gods I deal with on a regular basis," she said, with a small laugh. "When everyone around you is a killer, what does it serve you to be a victim? You must become the most dangerous of killers."

"Kill or be killed?" I asked. "Survival of the deadliest?"

She sighed and looked off to the side for a few seconds.

"You cannot possibly comprehend my world, Simon," she said. "Did you know that I am feared, not only in my pantheon, but in several others as well? As much as I am feared, I am also ostracized."

"You?"

"Oh, they don't do it overtly," she said, with a short laugh that sounded dangerous. "They fear me too much for that. So we play an elaborate game of forgotten invitations and insults by proxy. Everyone is very formal to your face while they brandish blades behind their backs. It's very tiresome, irritating and to be frank, quite vapid."

"That gives new meaning to a cut-throat environment," I said. "Is that why you cursed me?"

"You know why I cursed you," she said after a moment.

"You disrupted a five-thousand year-old plan. I nearly atomized you in that moment."

"Let's put a pin in the atomizing idea," I said. "I want to ask you a question, but atomizing, maiming and the inflicting of any pain has to be off the table as a response."

"This must be some question. Ask."

"This five-thousand year-old plan, how did you not plan for the possibility of someone like me interfering and messing it all up?" I asked. "I mean, after five millennia, I'm the one that screws up this plan?"

"That question is the right question," she said. "Why do you think Shiva hired you? He could have chosen any number of detective agencies in the city, yet he selected yours. Do you know why?"

"My excellent credentials?"

"Hardly," she said. "Even before my curse, which you shouldn't have survived, by the way, you possessed singular qualities. These qualities made you the ideal candidate for what you are currently undergoing as my Marked One."

"Qualities you aren't going to share at the moment?"

"Did you seek me out to talk about yourself?" she asked, raising an eyebrow. "I do have other matters to attend to."

"I'm going to take that as a no."

"Correct," she said. "You have a request, make it."

"I need to speak to Iris."

"Iris?" she asked mildly surprised. "Whatever for?"

"You didn't answer my question about Dira," I said. "Why do you want me to assist her? She wants to kill me."

"I'm aware," she said. "I also think you should end her before she ends you."

"I know."

"You think me harsh and cold?"

"No, well, yes, that *is* harsh and cold," I said. "But I get your way of thinking, I think. In order for me to be the best Marked of Kali, I need to demonstrate that I'm the best."

"And why should you help her?"

"Because the introduction of Chandra breaks your rules somehow," I said, giving it thought. "It gives Dira an unfair advantage."

"No, I want you to help her, because if she is to kill you she must do so on her own merits, not with the assistance of a deranged Blood Hunter and using my assassin's blade," she said. "As a successor, she has everything she needs to end your existence."

"Isn't it a little unfair, considering your curse?" I asked. "She can't kill me permanently without unfair assistance."

"It doesn't preclude the abilities she possesses," Kali said. "She only needs to successfully kill you to become one of my Marked. I never said anything about you staying dead, or being the only Marked One."

I thought back and realized she was right. Not that I was in any hurry to get dead. But I never considered that Kali could have more than one Marked One.

It made sense when I thought about it. She had many successors and Kali had never said there could be only one Marked. It would stand to reason that there were many Marked Ones out there.

"You never pointed out that little detail," I said. "How many Marked Ones are there?"

"Two things," she said, holding up two fingers. "I don't need to explain things to you. Ever. And the number of Marked Ones who exist will become apparent to you over time. As you grow in strength, they too will seek you out."

"In the end there can be only one?"

"What? That's nonsense," she scoffed. "The Marked Ones form a fighting unit designed to reinforce the Blades of Kali and take on other covert operations. What will only one serve?"

"Sorry, I got a little carried away there."

"There is one thing that makes you unique," she said. "You are the only Marked One who bears my curse. As such, you are poised to lead them should you choose to do so. In any case, as the current *perceived* leader, every successor will challenge you."

"Current perceived leader?" I asked. "Since when? I don't want to lead a unit of Marked Ones."

"One of the reasons you were chosen is because you do not seek it out," she said. "As for why you are the perceived leader, I may have let it slip that you are currently the one to destroy, if anyone wants the position."

"The Marked One must be tested?"

"Precisely," she said. "Now, why Iris? I could tell you where Dira is and you could go confront her, convince her to give you the blade, and she can proceed to attempt to kill you as a proper successor should."

I stared at her for a few seconds.

"You're serious?"

"Simon, it's not that I lack the ability to jest, it's that my jests are always taken poorly," she said. "No one understands my humor."

"I can only imagine," I said, and shook my head. "No, I want to do this with Iris."

"Why?"

"Because she wields a blade like mine and Esti managed to steal it," I said. "I want to know how and why she let Esti live."

"I can help you with this."

I raised a hand.

"Your help isn't really the kind of *help* I want, thanks," I said. "Besides, now that we have an understanding, it's made a few things clear."

"Such as?"

"You're not my friend and never were," I said. "I don't even think you understand the concept of friendship, not real friendship. I think it has something to do with you being *nirguna*—beyond all qualities of nature, and transcendent."

"You have been studying," she said with a slight nod. "You are correct. The human concept of friendship escapes me and seems frivolous. Gods do not have friends."

"I'm getting that," I said. "I can have Iris locate Chandra, and with that information confront Dira and give her the opportunity to return the blade to Iris."

"Or die an honorable death."

"Or die an honorable death," I said. "It's not Dira I'm really concerned about here. I need to stop Esti and this Sanguinary Order, before she unleashes something worse than a Demogre on the city."

"Stop?" Kali asked. "I suggest something more permanent than stopping her."

"Agreed. I also need to speak to Valentina, who is currently leading the Blood Hunters," I said. "I'm not trying to start a Vampire-Blood Hunter war in the city."

"You will seek her permission?"

"No," I said. "I don't *need* her permission to put Esti down, she's not a Blood Hunter, at least not anymore. I'm just giving her notice that if she unleashes her Blood Hunters on me or mine over whatever happens with Esti, we *will* go to war."

Kali gave me a slight nod.

"I approve," she said. "Iris will meet you in your home at the rising of the next sun on your plane."

The clouds began closing in on us.

A few seconds later, she was completely hidden and I felt

a sudden shift in movement. When the clouds disappeared, we were back at the campus. Sitting next to me, were two large sausages. I warily examined them, remembering the last time Kali provided my hellhound with some meat.

<Don't eat those yet, boy.>

<The blue lady is good, can I eat them now?>

<No, the last time Kali made you sausages they were spiked with some kind of cast. Don't you remember?>

<I remember they were delicious. Can I eat them now?>

<No, we wait for Monty to check them out first. Then you can eat them.>

My hellhound looked around, sniffed the air and looked around again.

<What are you doing?>

<Locating the angry man. I will bring him here.>

He sniffed the air again as I raised an arm.

"No, you don't have to—"

It was too late, Peaches had blinked out.

TWENTY

I remained on the bench and waited.

A few minutes later, my hellhound reappeared with a slightly disheveled Monty in tow.

"I see he found you," I said, pointing to the sausages. "Courtesy of Kali."

"Ah, that explains it," Monty said. "I take it you would like me to examine these in case they bear some kind of enhancements?"

"I'd like to avoid a repeat of the last time Kali made meat for my ever-hungry hellhound," I said. "Can you check them?"

Peaches sat in front of the sausages as Monty gestured causing a golden glow to come over his hands. He picked up each of the sausages and let the glow from his hands completely cover them.

After about a minute, he shook his head.

"They seem to be regular sausages," he said. "Of course we're dealing with a goddess. Her ability completely transcends mine and she could have placed any number of hidden casts inside this meat."

"She wouldn't try to hurt him," I said looking at my

drooling hellhound. "Plus if I tell him he can't eat them, it will end his world, look at him."

Monty glanced down at my hellhound and shook his head.

"I suggest you let him eat them before we end up standing in a pool of his saliva," he said, stepping back from Peaches. "What did your goddess say?"

"Iris will be at the Moscow at dawn tomorrow," I said. "Why don't gods use watches? She couldn't have said eight o'clock or something like that? She needs to go with dawn?"

"They occasionally reject technology, preferring to rely on trusted sources of timekeeping," he said. "The sun has proven fairly reliable for ages. She was using what was most familiar."

"I get it. Did you formulate a plan with the Morrigan?"

"Yes, but I have one question," he said. "Why didn't you have Kali assist you with this? I mean more than putting you in touch with Iris. She could have summoned Dira to any location or used you as bait and had Dira come to a location of your choosing."

"We're still doing something like that," I said. "I just don't want to involve Kali any more than we have to. Trust me, you don't want her *help*."

"I don't?" he asked. "What exactly does Kali's help entail?"

"The stuff of nightmares," I said. "You ready to head back?"

He nodded.

"My uncle Dexter won't be back for some time," he said. "The Morrigan will contact me when he returns. He will want us to join him on the next phase of Project Icarus."

"Project Icarus?" I said. "As in wax wings and flying too close to the sun? That Icarus?"

"Yes, it's what he plans to do with Haven, the Pit and Salius," Monty said looking off in the direction of the Menagerie. "Apparently he has some grand design in mind that incorporates them all. I don't know all the details yet."

"Speaking of Haven," I said. "Are you going to reach out to Roxanne?"

"We spoke briefly while I was with the Morrigan, who was kind enough to facilitate our conversation."

"How angry is she?"

"You say that like there is some scale I can use to measure her levels of anger," he said, dodging the question. "If I had to hazard a guess I would say it would be in our best interests not to visit Haven for the foreseeable future."

"We left the Dark Goat there."

"Cecil will retrieve it and deliver it to the Moscow."

I nodded.

"But you're going to have to see her...eventually."

"It won't be at Haven," Monty said, shaking his head. "We'll meet in the Randy Rump's back-room with reinforced null runes in place."

"Smart man," I said. "Let's head back. I don't think Iris is the kind of person we should keep waiting. How soon til dawn?"

"We have a fair amount of hours," he said. "Why?"

"Let's go pay Valentina a visit," I said. "And I need to get in touch with Chi. If Esti and the Heretics of the Sanguinary Order are gunning for me, they're gunning for her too."

"That is not the most prudent course of action," Monty said, walking over to a large green circle etched into the stone. "Attacking the former Director is a guaranteed way to invite an early death."

"I agree," I said, stepping into the circle, "but this is the Sanguinary Order, vampires don't faze them. They've been at this for how long?"

"They are much older than the Blood Hunters with methods considered cruel and barbaric as part of their regular arsenal."

"They also use darkmages," I said. "Blood Hunters don't use darkmages."

"That we know of," Monty said. "It hasn't made them any less effective. They nearly killed your vampire, twice."

"That's why we're paying Valentina a visit."

"You plan on threatening them? Or is this a courtesy visit?"

"Both?" I said. "I want to speak to Valentina face-to-face."

"Because that will make her quake in her boots?"

"Because I want to look into her eyes when I promise her a war that will wipe out every Blood Hunter in the city if she retaliates against Chi for what we're going to do to Esti."

"I imagine Valentina has distanced herself from Esti and the Heretics of the Order."

"You know what I didn't get?"

"What?" he said, touching the edge of the circle and sending a stream of green energy around the circle. "Are we expecting something from the Blood Hunters?"

"I didn't get a heads up or a call or anything from Valentina, regarding Esti and her new group of friends at the Order," I said following the stream of green energy with my gaze. "Her silence makes her complicit with Esti's actions."

"We don't want to start *that* war, at least not yet," Monty said as the energy made the circuit. "That would involve the entire Dark Council."

"Then I guess we better have this conversation sooner, rather than later," I said "We have some words with Valentina and remind her of our pact, then meet with Iris."

The circle filled with green energy and pulsed three times before shifting us away from the School of Battle Magic.

TWENTY-ONE

We arrived inside our apartment in the Moscow.

"We still have a few hours before Iris gets here," I said. "Why did we come here?"

"Change of clothes," he said, giving me a stink-eye. "We won't have time to pause a battle to get reinforced clothing. I, for one, need to change and possibly destroy this suit. You should definitely consider burning what you're wearing."

"What's wrong with what I'm wearing?" I said, looking down at my clothes. "I'm perfectly comfortable with what I have on."

"That is the problem," he said, heading to his section of the living area. "Consider upgrading to one of the suits Piero gave you. They're all runed and you'll present an image that's not a scruffy, nearly homeless New Yorker."

"I'll look like a mage if I wear one of those suits," I grumbled, heading to my area. "I don't want to look like a mage."

"Image matters," Monty called out. "Valentina may take you more seriously if you demonstrate that you have upgraded your clothing selection. Also it's an unspoken statement, clothes make the man."

"That sounds suspiciously like you're trying to Bard me," I said. "Dress well because apparel oft proclaims the man. Sounds very familiar."

"Polonius to Laertes, yes, Hamlet," Monty confirmed. "Shakespeare was, as he often is, correct. Let your clothing do the talking for once and we may even leave the Blood Hunters without bloodshed."

"Doubtful, but we can always dream," I said. "Fine, I'll make Piero happy. I'm sure he'd love to see me in one of his full suits."

"If I'm not mistaken, you have a runed Zegna. A dark blue Oasi Cashmere that he selected just for you," he said. "Wear that. You should still be able to fight in it, if the need arises."

I looked in my closet and found the suit he was referring to. I had to admit it looked impressive, especially with the subtle runes that were visible throughout the fabric.

"Okay," I said, pulling out the suit. "I'm sold on the suit, but—"

"Next to it, should be the Zegna shirt in indigo, also runed and chosen for you," he finished. "Piero knows what he is doing. I'm aware of your dislike of ties, which is why Piero didn't provide any."

"Ties are just nooses waiting to hang you," I said. "I never understood the assassins or agents who are shown wearing ties. Tell me you want to get choked and killed without actually telling me."

"An excellent point," he said. "I'm not overly fond of them either."

"Tell me you're not wearing the same thing I'm wearing," I called out again. "We are not doing the twin thing."

"Don't be ridiculous. House Zegna has made me an entirely different set of suits, which Piero has runed," he said. "Don't forget to check your ammunition. If we are facing a Demogre, it wouldn't hurt to bring conventional weaponry."

"Good idea," I said. "Do you think Peaches will be able to fight the Demogre? I don't want him to get hurt."

"I have yet to observe anything we have faced that can do any lasting damage to your hellhound," he said. "He's been exploded, thrown, launched, crushed, slapped, punched, flamed, and impacted with various blunt objects and weapons. He has managed to not only survive them all, but offer us protection in the midst of all these attacks."

"We've never faced a Demogre."

"True."

"Is it possible that a nullifying field could make Peaches weak, and then he could get hurt?"

"Demogres were created as a counter to mages," he said. "I don't know if the Demogre's negating qualities would work on your hellhound. While he qualifies as a being of magic, he doesn't use magic. I suppose there's only one way to find out."

"That's what I'm afraid of," I said. "If he gets nulled, the Demogre will have him for lunch."

"Hellhounds are resilient and nearly indestructible," he said. "I'll add that your hellhound in particular, has also withstood facing a dragon, more than once, and survived standing against his father. I think hellhounds get stronger when they are bonded. You'd have to ask Hades."

"Pass," I said, with a growl. "I've exceeded my 'speaking with gods' quota for the year, thank you."

"Things not go well with Kali?"

"They went as I expected," I said, with a slight shudder at the images she so generously shared with me. "She felt the need to educate me about my curse, and as usual, used the worse possible method available to do so."

"Kali, it *was* Kali, yes?"

"Yes, blue skin, extra arms, red tongue, and a large dose of fearsome," I said. "That Kali, yes."

"Well she isn't exactly known for her pleasant and gentle

manner," he said. "Other gods and pantheons give her a wide berth. It's not for her charms and easy going manner."

"I guess I should expect as much from anyone who has *the Destroyer* as an official part of their name."

"A definite indicator as to their demeanor," he said. "That's another good reason to learn more about your battleform and the bond with your creature."

"Really? Why? So Peaches and I can stand against Kali?" I said, giving him a look. "Are you listening to yourself right now?"

"Granted, it wouldn't be the most prudent course of action."

"A short-lived suicide attempt is what it would be," I said. "The amount of power she wields...I don't even have the words to describe what it would mean to face her. She wouldn't even break a sweat separating Peaches and me into molecules. No thanks. To infinity and beyond."

"Regardless, you still need to speak to Hades," he said. "He is the best source when it comes to knowing about hellhounds."

"He's the *only* source."

"You do have a point there, but I still prefer not to speak to him about this right now."

"The conversation is inevitable."

"But not now," I said. "Hades always has a reason for the things he does...always."

"Be that as it may, an in-depth conversation with him about hellhounds and bondmates is in order," he said. "Especially now that you are learning the battleform."

I hated that he was right.

"Fine, while we're at it, we can also go check out Orethe's place in the Underworld," I said. "May as well take an inventory and see what she left me."

"It's not Orethe's place any longer," he said. "It's yours."

He let the words hang there for a few seconds.

"That's going to take some getting used to," I said. "Let's just call it Orethe's for now. That okay with you?"

"Yes, yes it is. Your suggestion is excellent. We can do an extensive inventory of the property and discuss hellhounds with Hades," he said. "If possible, maybe even take some time off."

"Careful," I said, as I got dressed. "That sounds dangerously close to what I would call a vacation."

"We can't take a vacation," he said. "Not for lack of desire, but lack of opportunity."

"I call BS," I said, finishing off my Zegna ensemble with a pair of Zegna black leather Torino loafers. I took a look in the mirror and shuddered at how different I looked. "I feel like I should be saying my name is Strong, Simon Strong."

"You're not quite English enough to pull *that* off," he said, walking into my area wearing a Black Trofeo Zegna bespoke mageiform that made the suit I was wearing look like casual wear. "Ian Fleming would turn in his grave if you attempted that, let's not. However, I must say, the suit, suits."

"You're not looking too shabby yourself," I said. "I mean you don't quite have that New York swagger that comes naturally to me, but I'll let it pass."

"Very gracious of you," he said, forming a large teleportation circle under us. "I've sent Cecil a message, to make sure the Dark Goat is in the garage when we return from the Blood Hunters."

Peaches padded over to where I stood and for the first time ever, did not try to dislocate any of my body parts. Maybe there was some truth to this wearing a suit thing Monty was talking about.

‹You didn't bump into me like you usually do, boy.›
‹You look nice. I didn't want to break your clothes. Maybe later

after you break them, I will help you finish, like the angry man always does with his clothes.>

"Do you know where the Blood Hunters are headquartered now?" I asked. "I doubt they would advertise something like that."

"The Blood Hunters are scattered all over the city in cells, functioning similar to a terrorist organization," he said. "However, unlike a terrorist organization, Valentina has a fixed location of operation."

"Either she is tactically naive or she is letting her enemies know she doesn't fear them and they know where they can find her if they want to spill blood."

"Aside from your pact, which was a result of your oath, they seem to have struck similar agreements with other organizations in the city," he said. "I believe they were allowed sanctuary status as long as they didn't go to war with the vampire faction of the Dark Council."

"How did they pull that off?"

"Dark Council vampires are off-limits," he said. "Any other vampire I imagine is fair game."

"Chi isn't going to let that go on for long," I said. "It makes her resignation from the Council a little clearer now. She did say she was stepping down to make the city safer for her kind."

"Blood Hunters present a considerable threat while they are in the city alongside vampires," Monty said. "I would imagine she would like to rectify that situation."

"She said she was going to invite them to vacate the city."

"I have a feeling that invitation will be declined," Monty said shaking his head. "Once she starts inviting them to vacate this life, it will start a war."

"I got the impression that didn't concern her too much," I said. "It's why she cut ties with the Dark Council. This will be a war of the Blood Hunters against one vampire."

"One fearsome vampire who can stand against the Blood Hunters," he said. "We need to see, and by we, I mean you, if it's possible to stave off this war."

"That would require a long, well longer, conversation with Chi," I said. "The last time we discussed this topic, we didn't end it on an encouraging note."

"You need to convince her a war is in no one's best interest right now," he said. "Especially one that will debilitate the Dark Council. Whatever she does, the Blood Hunters will retaliate against the Council."

"I tried explaining that to her," I said. "You think she doesn't know that? Having the Blood Hunters in her city is unacceptable. She's not budging on that point."

"Perhaps Valentina can be convinced to relocate?" he said. "Imminent death has a way of motivating people."

I nodded.

"Let's go talk to Valentina," I said. "What's the worst she can say, no ?"

He gestured and the circle bloomed to life with green energy. We stepped into the circle and left the Moscow behind as a wave of green energy washed over us.

TWENTY-TWO

We arrived at 86th and Henderson Place.

It was a series of connected townhouses I could only describe as quaint and homey. It looked more suited to a quiet street in some English neighborhood, a fairly expensive and posh English neighborhood, than on the east side of the city.

We actually stood across from the property and when I looked closer, I realized why. On the two corners adjacent to 86th Street, I saw Blood Hunter sentries.

Across the roof, I noticed more sentries standing guard. They were using some sort of camouflage that prevented them from being easily seen.

All of the Blood Hunters on the roof carried crossbows.

"Either I'm seeing things, or there are sentries all over that property," I said. "Is that why we teleported here instead of inside?"

"Had I teleported inside, which would have been quite difficult considering the defenses on the property, it would have been interpreted as an act of war," Monty said. "This property, after their arrangement, is treated similarly to Julien's home. It is sovereign soil."

"If Chi attacks this place…"

"It would be a phenomenally horrible idea," he said, as we crossed the street. "The Dark Council would have to publicly renounce her actions and even dispatch Enforcers to apprehend the Director."

"She's not the Director anymore."

"Apologies, apprehend the rogue vampire who attacked the Blood Hunters without provocation—on their own soil."

"I doubt she would consider it without provocation," I said, keeping my gaze wide in case the sentries on the roof decided I needed some arrows to go with my ensemble. "Blood Hunters and vampires have been at war for a long time. For Chi, an attack would be long overdue."

Peaches matched my pace as we reached the Blood Hunter's property, but I could tell he was tense. He gave off a low rumble as we approached the sentry on the corner.

<Easy, boy. We're just going in there to talk.>

<I do not think they want to talk.>

"We would like an audience with Valentina Mikaela Santiago," Monty said, flexing the formality. "I was informed she was in?"

The sentry turned to face us completely as did several of the Blood Hunters on the roof above. If anything went sideways we were going to get perforated with blood arrows at what felt like point-blank range.

The entire group of homes on this corner were only four, or at most, five stories tall. We were easy targets at this range and I knew from experience, some of them could actually shoot.

"Tell her Simon Strong is here to speak with her," I said before Monty could say more. I didn't want him to get too wrapped up in Blood Hunter insanity. Besides, I was the one who made the pact with Valentina and I was the one who held one of the blood blades they wanted back—Ebonsoul. "She knows who I am."

The sentry, who was dressed in casual, black combat armor looked me over and then let her eyes settle on mine.

"*Si*," she said. "We all know who you are, *asesino*. Wait here."

She nodded to the other sentries and climbed the small stoop to enter the corner property. The other sentry at the far corner came over to take her place and gave me a massive dose of stink-eye.

"*Asesino?*" Monty said. "I believe that means—"

"Killer," I said. "I know what it means. They're just giving me a not-so-friendly reminder about Anastasia."

"Indeed," he said. "It would seem the Blood Hunters have long memories."

"They hunt vampires," I said, keeping my voice low. "I wouldn't expect anything less."

The first sentry reappeared after a few minutes and motioned for us to come in. She held the door open as we climbed the stone steps and stepped into a large foyer.

"I was informed to remind you of your pact," she said, with a slight accent. "You are standing on the soil of the Blood Hunters' domain. Everything and anything you say or do while a guest of the *Cazadoras de Sangre*, will reflect upon all those you hold dear."

I nodded.

"Understood," I said. "I will honor my pact."

"If you don't, I will be one of the first to let my blade taste your blood," she said, looking at me. "Remember that."

"Noted," I said, taking a deep breath and letting it out slowly. It was going to be a challenge to deal with all the angry

Blood Hunters looking to avenge Anastasia's death. "Is it your job to take us to Valentina, or to not so subtly threaten me? Or is it both? I just want to understand if the threats are going to be a feature of the upcoming guided tour?"

Monty shook his head and the sentry glared at me as her face flushed a deep crimson.

"This way," she said, and led us deeper into the home. "Valentina is waiting."

We walked through the expansive property, which was richly furnished with mostly dark colored woods and stone. Even at night, the many windows made the interior feel open and wide. At integral at choke points, like doorways and the windows, I could see all the runes.

They took their security seriously.

I noticed as she led us through the complex that although they appeared to be separate homes from the outside, inside, all the homes were connected with common areas and corridors that joined them together.

After several minutes of walking through the space, the sentry led us down a small staircase into a sunken area, which appeared to serve as a main reception area of sorts.

At the other end of the reception area was a large, wooden door that looked like Buloke, but I wasn't certain.

"Monty, that door, is it—?"

"Australian Buloke? Yes, or a variant of it," he said with a nod. "The runes etched on the surface make the area behind it the most secure room in this entire complex."

"Valentina's office?"

"Or her stronghold," he said. "No one is getting through that door without a massive expenditure of power. It's comparable to the door in the backroom of the Randy Rump."

I nodded and gazed at the door again.

Was it a show of power? Or was Valentina taking the necessary precautions because she didn't want to share Anastasia's fate?

Only one way to find out.

TWENTY-THREE

The sentry led us to the door and knocked.

I looked up and noticed several of the cameras situated all around the room. Every angle was covered. After a few seconds, the door hissed open and the sentry pulled on the large door.

"Hydraulic locks," I said under my breath to Monty. "Impressive."

"And nearly impossible to circumvent, no one gets in this room unless Valentina allows it, it seems."

With the door fully open, the sentry stepped back to allow us to step inside, then. She closed the door behind us. The door whispered shut with a much lower hiss this time.

"I know this may be pointless but it doesn't hurt to ask," I said. "Can you get through this door if you had to?"

"You recall my earlier comment about certain actions being perceived as acts of war?" he asked. "Trying to forcibly open this door would be at the top of that list, right after physically attacking the leader of the Blood Hunters or any of those in her employ."

"What if they attack us first?"

"Then you had better be able to prove it with irrefutable evidence," a female said from the side. "Do you think you can? Will it even matter? If you launch an attack, all of the Blood Hunters in this complex will—"

"I know," I said, raising a hand. "Let their blades taste my blood. The guide made sure I understood how much of a fan she was."

"It was not an idle threat, Strong," Valentina said, as we turned to face her. "Every Blood Hunter on this property would want nothing more than to end your life."

That was going to be difficult to pull off, but I didn't share that with her.

"Taking the Blood Hunters on would be pointless," I said, shaking my head. "Attempting something like that would only bring a world of pain down on us."

"You speak truth," she said. "Good evening, Mage Montague. Well met."

"Well met, Blood Hunter Santiago," Monty said, with a slight bow. "I see the Blood Hunters have established themselves well in the city. The pacts with the authorities are holding?"

"There is some friction, but nothing we didn't expect."

"Are they allowing you to hunt within the confines of the city?"

"Only those the Dark Council deem rogue, which is a substantial number," she answered. "For now, it is an acceptable agreement."

She was wearing typical Blood Hunter gear, black armor, but slightly modified I imagined for everyday wear. As I examined her armor, I realized how similar it was to the Daystrider armor vampires wore to travel during the day and protect themselves from the sun.

I kept that information to myself.

No need to kick a hornet's nest when I was standing right in the middle of it, maybe I'd kick it on the way out.

The office and living space we stood in was, like the rest of the property, a mix of rustic and modern. It was half functional office and half living area designed to entertain guests.

Valentina walked over to her desk and I got the message. We weren't welcome, but we would be tolerated…for now.

She sat behind her desk and placed both hands on its surface, palms down. She leaned back slightly and focused on me for a few seconds before raising an eyebrow at my clothing.

"I see you've learned some fashion sense from the mage," she said. "You actually look respectable. Now, tell me why you're here."

"I need to stop Estilete."

"Don't you mean kill?"

"If you know of another way to stop her, I'm open to it."

"How magnanimous," she said, with a smile that never reached her eyes. "You killed Anastasia."

"In battle."

"Which is the only reason why you're still breathing. Because of you and your actions, Estilete lost everything. Sadly, I think that includes her mind as well."

"She was unstable even before we met."

"You took her arm, her standing, and the one person she admired, respected, and loved," Valentina said. "Are you surprised she wants to destroy you?"

"No. Is she still one of yours?" I asked. "Do you still consider her a Blood Hunter?"

"She stopped being a Blood Hunter the moment she joined *La Orden Sanguinaria*—The Sanguinary Order. She is beyond saving now."

"She attacked me earlier."

"She must be slipping, since you're standing here telling

me this, and I'm not hearing about your death from another source."

"She unleashed a Demogre," I said, watching her face for any reaction. She narrowed her eyes and flexed the muscles of her jaw. Other than that, she was unreadable. "Did you know she could do that?"

"She must be moving in different circles these days," she said, her face expressionless. "Did you come here to give me a report of her activities?"

"I came here to inform you that she stole a weapon from Iris—the leader of the Blades of Kali—and gave that weapon to an enemy of mine," I said and I saw fear flit across her expression. "I'm meeting with Iris at dawn. I'm going to find this person, take back the weapon and return it to its owner. In the process, if Esti crosses my path—"

"You know she will."

"Then I will end her," I said. "I wanted you to hear it from me first. Will this shatter our pact?"

"And if it does?"

"I'm prepared for that outcome if it comes to it," I said. "I don't want a war with you or the Blood Hunters, but I'm not running. Are you ready to lose your Hunters?"

"Are you ready to lose those you hold dear?"

"No," I said, thinking about the images Kali shared with me. "No, I'm not, and I will fight until my last breath to protect them. Trust me when I say you don't want to find out how far that is."

"The blood oath between us is a stronger bond than the one Estilete broke in her pursuit of your destruction," she said. "The Blood Hunters have no quarrel with you, nor do we wish to start a war with the Marked of Kali."

"How did you—?"

"*Es sabiduria permancer informada,*" she said. "Don't you agree?"

"It *is* wisdom to remain informed, "I answered. "I just didn't expect that news to be broadcasted anywhere."

"We hunt the undead, we have ways of learning even the most hidden things," she said. "I do have one request."

"Yes?"

"I ask that when you face her, be merciful, make her end quick."

"I will."

"I take it we have nothing else to discuss?"

"Michiko."

"Is our sworn enemy and has been for centuries," she said her voice hard. "Nothing you say or propose can or will change that. I realize your position, and I accept that one day, we will face each other across a battlefield. Until then, nothing will be altered. I am aware she resigned her position as Director of the Dark Council."

"She did, yes."

"Do you know why?"

"To hunt you."

"You are partially correct," she said. "She resigned to allow the Council to designate her a rogue. She did it so we could hunt her as well and not involve the Dark Council.

"I see."

"Think long and hard before you involve yourself in the whirlwind of death that sits between us, Strong" she said. "You may find yourself regretting that decision when the day comes."

"I'll do my best to make sure that day never comes."

"This dance began before either of us stepped onto the floor," she said, with a sad smile and shook her head. "Still, a small part of me hopes that you will succeed in that dream. If there is nothing else?"

"No, nothing," I said. "Do you want me to inform you—?"

"We will know," she said. "Remember my request."

"I will."

She placed her hand on a section of her desk and a red teleportation circle formed on the floor behind where we stood.

"That will take you outside. Remember your pact and keep the blade safe," she said. "We will see you soon."

Monty and I nodded and gave her a slight bow before stepping into the circle. Peaches stepped close to me, rumbled and nearly shoved me out of the circle.

The circle flashed with red energy and Valentina and the Blood Hunters headquarters was gone.

TWENTY-FOUR

We stood outside across the street from the Blood Hunters' home.

"We should've had Cecil drop the Dark Goat off here," I said. "You plan on making a circle out on the street?"

"No, even though it's late, it may attract too much attention," Monty said. "Let's go across the street to the park."

"Your circles are usually flashy affairs. Won't it attract too much attention, even in there?" I asked. "We could always take the subway or hail a cab."

"The subway is best avoided at certain hours," he said, cryptically. "And I don't seem to see any taxis to hail, do you?"

"Well, considering the hour and the fact that if we go any farther east, we will be in the East River, the chances of finding a cab are slim to none."

"True," he said, looking up and down East End Avenue. "This area is quite desolate at this hour."

"Plus, there is no cabbie in this city who will take us as a fare, once they see my adorable hellhound," I added, as I patted Peaches on the head as we crossed the street and headed to Carl Schurz Park. "They're more likely to break the land-speed record trying to get away, once they see his smile."

"Teleportation circle it is, then," Monty said, flexing his fingers. "I should be able to construct one fairly easily near those trees."

"You sure?" I asked, looking at the trees and pointed. "It might be easier to use the promenade, it has some areas that are obscured."

He nodded.

We headed up the stairs and onto the wide promenade. The East River flowed below and in front of us. To our sides, benches were evenly spaced out every few feet so visitors could sit and gaze out over the river.

"Hello, Strong," a voice said in the darkness. "I've been waiting for this moment."

Dira.

I didn't sense her in the slightest and the Morrigan's words came back to me: *You're not paying attention, in more ways than one. If I'm not hiding, what does that mean?*

I really needed to practice.

"Dira," I said, making sure there was space between us as I turned to face her. "It's been a while. You're looking especially homicidal tonight. Is that a new sword? What happened to your *Bas Magus*? This an upgrade?"

She glanced briefly at the blade she held. A wicked blade that looked sharp enough to slice through anything. She was dressed in her unique combat armor of red silk, except now there were black sections that looked reinforced.

Upgrades, wonderful.

"You like it?" she said, holding it up. "It's a kamikira, and designed to kill gods, I guess it will destroy someone as clueless as you." She turned to Monty. "Mage, if you so much as move a finger to make a gesture, I swear I will make the Marked of Kali suffer long and hard before he dies."

Monty raised his hands so she could see them. Not that that meant anything. He could gesture from any position. He gave her a short nod and glanced at me, letting me know he would let me handle it until it was necessary to jump in and maybe drop another building on her.

Except, as I looked around, I realized that all of the buildings were a good distance behind us. We could probably launch her into the river, or I could have Peaches blink her out of there, but it was too risky while she was holding Chandra.

The sword appeared to be a longer version of Ebonsoul and reminded me of Grey's blade. It was black and covered in red runes, which pulsed in the night.

I could feel the power it gave off and noticed that Dira, although she felt powerful, was off somehow. She felt sick, as if the power coursing through her body was breaking her down slowly.

Her energy signature had increased, but she looked like she was running a fever. Her face was drawn and pale, and I could see the micro tremors in the hand that held the blade. There was no way she could face me in this condition...and live.

Chandra was killing her.

I needed her to let go of the sword and give it to me or least give it a try. That way, when Kali unleashed the pain, I could at least say I gave it a shot.

I knew I couldn't let her leave here with that sword. I was noticing there were little to no upsides to being the Marked of Kali.

Time to try some tact and diplomacy. I would approach this from the side instead of head on and make her see reason. If that failed, I could always stab her with Ebonsoul to make my point...in more ways than one.

I cleared my throat and focused on her.

"How long were you tracking us?" I asked. "I didn't sense you."

Show some weakness. Get her to relax her guard.

"Long enough to know you need practice," she said, looking around and sniffing the air. "Where are the dead creatures? Do you have them hiding in the trees?"

"Dead creatures?" I asked. "What are you talking about?"

"I think she means the shamblers," Monty said. "They were pursuing you the last time you two met." He turned to her. "They have been dispatched along with the revenant."

She stared at me.

"Is this true?" she asked. "Show me your arms."

"Pushy much?" I said. "What if I don't want to?"

"I could always remove them at the elbow and look for myself," she said. "I want to know if you are still a sick dog."

"You really have a way with words," I said, baring my arms to her. "See? No poison, I'm healed. You on the other hand, are not looking too good."

Peaches rumbled by my side and entered shred-and-maim mode as his eyes flashed with power.

"I know you want to keep your demon dog alive," she threatened, pointing Chandra at him. "Keep him under control, or I will end him."

My initial reaction was to cut right through her for threatening my hellhound, but I restrained myself. I took a deep breath and let it out slowly.

"His name is Peaches, not demon dog," I said with an edge. "If you don't threaten him or any of us, he won't attack you. If you can't control yourself, he'll rip parts off of you faster than you can imagine. Your call."

She nodded and lowered Chandra.

"You are healed, good," she said, ignoring my comment, but still keeping a wary eye on Peaches. "This means it's time to end your pitiful existence."

"Before we jump to the pain and maiming, I need to speak to you about that blade," I said. "You have to be feeling it. It's making you sick. No worse, it's killing you."

"You resort to lies to save your life," she scoffed. "You are not worthy of being the Marked of Kali."

"I understand where you're coming from, and what you want more than anything is to be *the* Marked One," I said in a reasonable tone. "It would really suck if you managed to kill me, only to have the *real* owner of that blade show up and dust you."

"The real owner?" she said. "This is a ruse. The owner was the one who gave me this blade."

"Wrong," I said. "The real owner is Iris, leader of the Blades of Kali. That name ring a bell?"

I figured she would know who Iris was, being a follower of Kali and all. Hopefully, if she knew that she was holding Iris's blade it would convince her to give it up before it destroyed her.

I shook my head at the irony. I was trying to save the person who'd made it her life's mission to kill me. Gods have a twisted sense of humor.

She took a step back at the mention of Iris's name.

"Impossible," she said, a tinge of fear in her voice. "The Blades of Kali are Kali's assassins. They cannot be defeated, they kill gods."

"I'm guessing that's what that blade is for," I said, pointing to Chandra. "I'm all for a major clash, but I'm going to meet Iris in"—I looked at my watch—"a few hours, at dawn. I was going to ask her to point me in your direction, but you saved me the trouble, thanks by the way."

"Why would Iris meet with you?" she snapped. "What reason could she have to speak to you?"

"You're holding it," I said. "Let's just say she's not exactly happy that someone managed to steal her blade. It makes her look bad, and I'm guessing she's not the type to let that kind of insult go unanswered. I think she's more the type to kill first and ask questions never. What do you think?"

"I think you would say anything to save yourself," she said, and hesitated for a moment. "But this blade is wrong. I thought I could control it, use it to kill you and then rid myself of it, but it's too strong."

I nodded.

"I'm willing to extend you the same courtesy you did to me when I was poisoned."

"What courtesy was this?"

"You refused to destroy me when I was, as you call it, a 'sick dog'," I said. "I appreciate the courtesy. You let me get well so you could kill me today. That was honorable. Let me be honorable in return."

"How? You have no concept of honor," she said. "You fear for your life and are using deceit to escape with your life."

"No," I said, materializing Ebonsoul. "I'm ready to do this, but I can guarantee you that the one-armed woman who gave you that sword is not the owner. She's a deranged ex-Blood Hunter who wants me dead."

"I never told you she was one-armed," Dira said. "How do you know this?"

"She set you up to meet Iris and get killed," I continued. "I don't know why. Maybe she doesn't want anyone else trying to kill me and wants to make sure she's the only one out here with the privilege of ending my life."

"She's your enemy?"

"Yes. I'm the reason she has single-handedly unleashed a shitstorm of epic proportions my way," I said. "I removed her arm. Her name is Esti and she's not exactly in her right mind."

"You removed her arm? You?" she asked, and looked at Ebonsoul. "Your blade, it's different. You are different."

"You're not the only one getting upgrades," I said. "Except that my blade doesn't come with a pissed off assassin standard. When Iris finds you, and she *will* find you, she won't be asking any questions. She will see you holding her sword, she'll take your life, and keep on moving. I can't believe I'm saying this: let me help you."

"Why?" she asked. "Why would you help *me*?"

"Kali wants me to help you," I said, shaking my head. "Don't ask me why. She thinks you don't need this blade to end my life. She said you have everything you need to do it yourself."

"She said this?"

"Yes," I said, looking around. "I'm not going to make up a conversation with a goddess who has 'the Destroyer' in her name. That sounds like suicide."

"And if I give you this blade, Iris will not seek retribution against me?" she asked. "You will speak with her on my behalf?"

I glanced at Monty, who gave me a slight shrug and a look that said: this one is all yours.

"Yes," I said, after a few moments. "I'll make sure Iris knows you had nothing to do with stealing her blade. Are you going to hand it over?"

"If you are lying to me—"

"You'll hunt me down and kill me?" I said. "Isn't that kind of what you want to do anyway? I have no reason to lie, we can fight to the death right now, if you want. The only thing that's keeping you from facing Iris in this moment, is Kali, who told her to hold off until I spoke to you, but hey, you want to do this, we can dance if you want to."

"Very well, Marked One," she said, placing the sword on the ground in an enormous display of trust. "When next we meet, I will end your existence."

She immediately began looking better.

"Looking forward to it," I said, glancing down at Chandra. "Nothing like impending death hanging over your head to make the days feel extra special."

"Jest while there is still breath in your lungs, Marked One," she said, her voice full of menace. "One day soon, it will be your last."

She took several steps back and disappeared without a trace.

I crouched down and looked at Chandra, which thrummed with enough power for me to feel it from a short distance. I absorbed Ebonsoul and stepped back.

"I'm not picking that thing up, it feels tainted."

"It's not designed for you," Monty said gesturing. "This is a weapon of malice, similar to Grey's Dark Spirit. If Dira had wielded it any longer—a few more days or a week, she would have been transformed into something else."

"Does that mean Ebonsoul is also a weapon of malice?"

"No," he said as he kept gesturing forming a golden lattice around Chandra. "Grey's blade is the home of Izanami. I'm fairly certain that is the primordial reason it's a weapon of malice. Also, don't forget, Grey is a powerful darkmage. He could probably wield this blade without ill effects."

"He's that strong?"

"Stronger," Monty said, completing the lattice around the blade. "I'm just going to put this in a pocket dimension similar to what I do with the Sorrows. It wouldn't do to lose this blade."

"Is it going to affect you, having it in there?" I asked. "I don't want you going Dark Monty on me. That wasn't fun the last time."

"I have never gone dark, and never will."

I shook my hand in a see-saw motion.

"I'd say you were dark around the fringes, maybe not full dark, but definitely on your way to utmost darkness," I said.

"Any darker and I was seriously considering calling you Darth Monty."

"Darth Monty?" he asked, as he gestured again and Chandra disappeared. I noticed he made a point not to touch the blade either. "That is an utterly ridiculous title."

"You only say that because you do not know the power of the dark side," I said. "And I, for one, am glad you don't."

"And never will."

"That was too close," I said as I moved over to a nearby bench and took several deep breaths, exhaling each of them slowly. "A few more days holding that sword and she was done, Dira wasn't looking too good. "

"No she wasn't, fortunately the corruption had not reached her mind," he said. "Had it taken hold, we would be fighting for our lives in this moment."

"I can't believe I was able to talk her down," I said, giving him a glance. "Maybe there is something to this tact and diplomacy thing we keep failing at. It worked this time."

"I must admit, I thought this would end differently."

"Same here," I said. "I just don't understand Kali, having me help Dira just so she can try to kill me later. The smart play would've been to let her die, or kill her here and now."

"You really think so?" he said, giving me a hard look. "Truly?"

I gave the situation some thought and realized that no, that wasn't who I was. Dira could think I had no concept of honor, but I was well-versed in the tenets of honor and being honorable. Killing her tonight would be the furthest thing from honor.

"No," I said simply. "It wouldn't be honorable."

"Perhaps Kali also felt it would be beneath the Marked of Kali to defeat an opponent in such a way," he added. "It could be why she gave you the task of saving the successor."

"Sure, so I could face her later when she tries to skewer

me ten different ways, just so she could become the Marked of Kali?"

"Do you think she could defeat you now?"

"The way she was today? No," I said. "Let's see where she is when we meet again."

"By the way, that was an excellent demonstration of tact," Monty said. "I suppose you'd like me to create the circle now?"

"I'd really appreciate that, yes," I said. "We give Iris her sword back and get Dira off the hook, that only leaves—"

"Esti," Monty said as he began forming the circle. "Do you have her number?"

I glared at him.

"Just make the circle," I said. "If we find the Demogre, we find Esti and the Order. I'm sure a mage of your caliber can pull that off."

"Quite right," he said, finishing the circle and activating it. "Let's get this sword back to its rightful owner."

"Let's," I said, "we still have a few hours."

We stepped into the circle and left Carl Schurz Park behind.

TWENTY-FIVE

We arrived back at the Moscow with some time before dawn.

Peaches padded over to the kitchen and rumbled. I reached into the large fridge we had to get just for hellhound meat and removed several pounds of Ezra's pastrami, placing it in a new industrial-sized titanium bowl inscribed with a large P, courtesy of Ezra.

"Here you go, boy," I said. "I'd hate for you to starve."

<You are the best bondmate I know.>

<I'm the only bondmate you know.>

<Which is why you are the best. Do you want to share some meat? It will make you strong and mighty.>

<Thank you, but I'll pass on the pounds of pastrami. Go ahead, knock yourself out.>

<Why would I want to lose consciousness? How would I eat my meat then?>

<Eat. Meat is life.>

<Yes, it is.>

Peaches chuffed at me and began the pastrami devouring session. I took a moment to really look at him and realized he was definitely growing. It was going to be a real concern when he became an adult hellhound. Would we even be able to walk down the street?

Granted, it shouldn't be much of an issue. There have been some insane things sighted on the streets of this city. One overly large, canine-looking creature wouldn't faze many people...unless he decided to smile.

Then I would probably get a call from Ramirez to stop terrorizing the citizens of his city. Speaking of, I needed to go pay him a visit. It had been too long.

I shook myself out of my reverie as Monty put a pot on.

The next moment, he gestured, materializing Chandra, and placing it on the counter near the kitchen without ever touching it.

"I see you're not a fan of touching it either," I said, noticing how he avoided handling it. "Is it the whole weapon of malice thing?"

"I'd rather not," he said. "Dealing with power above my level tends to skew the mind. I still recall how the First Elder Rune felt. It's not a feeling I wish to revisit."

"How do you want to deal with Iris?" I said, pulling out my flask. I reached for my Death Wish thermos and poured some of the inky black goodness into my favorite mug with a spoonful of javambrosia. Monty raised an eyebrow as I created the perfect coffee. "We just give her the sword and part ways?"

"I don't even know if Iris is human," Monty said. "I'm not well-versed in the Vedic pantheon. In the Hindu pantheon, Kali is the most compassionate goddess they have, even though she's known as the Goddess of Death."

"I'm going to say Kali chooses which pantheon she wants to represent depending on her mood," I said. "What does that have to do with Iris?"

"Well, if she is an assassin, she may feel gratitude for our participation in getting her weapon back though—"

"How she lost it in the first place still boggles my brain," I said. "How did Esti pull that one off?"

"I doubt it was Esti, I would hazard to say that whoever procured the Demogre, had a hand in stealing Iris's sword."

"Why do I feel like we're going to meet that person sooner or later," I said, taking a sip from my mug of delicious javambrosia goodness. "Mmm you really should consider giving up the soggy leaf water. This is the only time I would say—if only you knew the power of the dark side."

"I truly hope we meet the person behind the theft later, much later," he said, as his water began to boil. "As for stepping over to your dark side, I think I'll stick with the serenity of my leaf water over the hypercharged power of your javambrosia-infused bean water, thank you."

"You don't know what you're missing."

"Actually, I do. I'll respectfully decline," he said. "As I was saying, *if* this Iris is human—"

"I haven't been human in over a thousand years, mage," a voice said, coming from Dex's room. "My Mistress requested I be here at the dawning of this place."

"I'm going to guess that's not Dex?"

"Not in the slightest," Monty said, looking out of the window. "It's not dawn yet, is it?"

"Maybe she's a super punctual assassin?"

"I am early," she said, rounding the corridor and stepping into the space between the kitchen and the reception area. She raised an eyebrow. "You have my blade. How did you manage this?"

Iris could give Nan a run for her money in the scary warrior department. She stood about a foot taller than both Monty and me and wore a variation of the robes Durga wore.

She wore her hair loose, and her dark eyes fixed us both in place as she scanned the space. Her light skin was covered in designs that reminded me of henna tattoos, but these looked permanent.

Her robes were a burnt sienna brown and were tied around her waist with a belt made of what appeared to be interlocking, curved sickle blades. On both wrists, she wore an assortment of bracelets and bangles of gold and silver.

Her feet were bare, but around her ankles she wore anklets made of small bells, which were silent when she walked.

The first impression she made was not the leader of an assassin group, until I felt her energy signature. It matched the blade that was currently sitting on our counter. Fearsome and deadly.

I explained the whole situation about how Dira was being set up and Esti gave her the blade to get her killed.

"Even this Esti is a pawn," Iris said, taking her blade. It shifted colors as she placed her hand around the hilt and then it immediately transformed into a silver and golden bracelet around her wrist. "This is the work of the sorceress Caligo, she is the one who managed to take my bracelet and unlock the weapon within."

"Is this Caligo a member of the Sanguinary Order?" I asked, still not seeing the connection. "Why is she helping them?"

"The Sanguinary Order?" Iris said. "This goes beyond them. Caligo works for a demon named Rakta, a sworn enemy of my Mistress. There is much hidden in this you cannot see."

"I think I am beginning to understand," Monty said. "This demon, Rakta, wants to attack Kali, but can't do it outright, not while you wield your weapon."

"He is a fool. He misunderstands the power of my Mistress and thinks he can weaken her by soiling her reputation," Iris said. "As if Kali needs other gods."

"I'm going to say she's fairly good on her own."

Iris gave me a look.

"She is not good, she is Kali."

"That's what I meant," I said, raising a hand. "I meant she doesn't need any other god or goddess."

"You are her Marked One," she said, looking at me. "Now, this makes sense."

"It does?"

"Yes, this Esti is your enemy?"

"She wants me dead, yes."

"And Dira is a successor," Iris said putting it together. "Her role is to destroy and replace you."

"There might be a slight problem with that."

"Your curse, yes," she said, surprising me. "Do not be surprised, many gods know of your curse and hate you for it. Gods do not tolerate new immortals well. Has this not been explained to you?"

"Explained? No," I said. "There may have been hints here and there, but no one sat me down and explained this to me."

"You are not a child," she said, staring down at me with a frown. "Why would anyone need to explain what is so clear? The greater your power, the greater the power of your enemies. The more you grow, the more attention you attract. Did you think the Marked of Kali could hide?"

"Well, when you put it that way...yes, it's been explained to me," I said with a nod. "I just didn't think—"

"That the attention you would garner would be murderous?" she asked. "Kali is a hated goddess because she is feared by so many. The path you are on is a lonely one, not only because of your curse, but because of *who* cursed you."

"They are attacking him by proxy?" Monty asked. "If they kill him—?"

"Then they strike a blow against my Mistress," Iris said.

"It is no small thing to kill an immortal. It cannot be done with any weapon."

"That explains the theft of Chandra, but why use Esti and Dira?" I asked. "Why not come after me themselves?"

"To attack you directly would reveal their plan and my Mistress would respond directly," she said. "Two things they seek to prevent at all costs. A lion does not attack a kitten. They must use proxies to achieve the ends they seek, so they hide their actions and motives."

"They steal your sword, give it to Esti, who gives it to Dira," I said. "That sounds like a mistake."

"Yes," Iris admitted. "I believe the plan was to have this Esti use my sword against you. Caligo must have influenced that decision."

"I'm guessing she believed she could use the Demogre and Dira as a two-pronged attack," Monty said. "If Dira failed, the Demogre would succeed, and if both of them failed, Esti and the Heretics of the Order could be the failsafe."

"And if Esti and the Order failed?" I asked. "What's the contingency for that?"

"Then that would sanction Rakta to dispatch Caligo after you directly," Iris said. "You do not want that outcome at your current level of power."

"I don't want that outcome at *any* level of power," I said, raising my voice. "They're going through all of this just to kill me?"

"Does this surprise you?" she asked. "What did you think it meant to be the Marked of Kali? To be cursed alive by her? To be immortal?"

"I don't know. Not this."

"You must understand, you pose a significant threat, not now, but later, in the future when you grow in power," she said, resting a hand on my shoulder. "Do you know when is the best time to kill your enemy?"

"Not a question I give a lot of thought to, no."

"When they are a babe," she said. "When they have yet to grow into their power. When they themselves do not realize they are a threat. That is when you strike. Right now, you are a babe, but the power you hold is considerable. Enough for them to notice."

"But not enough to stop them on my own?"

"You are not on your own," she said, glancing at Monty and Peaches. "You have a mage brother and a hellhound bondmate. How are you alone? Together, you three have faced gods. There is much power in your unity and this is what they fear."

"Is it safe to assume this Rakta is behind the Demogre, being that he is a demon?" Monty asked. "Did he help Caligo?"

"Yes," Iris said. "He is the one who provided the demon to make the Demogre."

"I'm guessing this Rakta is way out of our league in terms of fighting him?" I asked. "We can't face him?"

"Can an ant face a dragon?" Iris asked. "It would be certain death."

"How *certain* exactly?" I said. "Can you put it in perspective? More reality and less metaphor?"

"Of course, I will speak plainly," she said. "Rakta battles against Kali and manages to escape with his life. What he lacks in power, he possesses in guile. You cannot stand against him, even I with Chandra, would find it difficult."

"Got it," I said. "We stay away from Rakta."

"A wise choice," she said. "Caligo is too strong for you alone, but together, you have a chance."

"Right now, we focus on Esti, the Order, and the Demogre," I said. "We leave the heavy hitters for another day."

"That day is coming sooner than you would like," she said. "I wish you all good fortune."

"Let me guess, you can't get involved the same way Caligo can't get involved," I said. "Not even to assist with the Demogre?"

"As much as I would enjoy that, it would escalate matters," she said, shaking her head. "Besides, this is good training for the Marked of Kali. Survive and become stronger. My Mistress thinks highly of her Marked One."

"She has a funny way of showing it," I said. "You can't help in any way?"

She looked away for a few moments.

"You did return my blade to me without bloodshed," she said. "And spared your successor a horrible death so that she may grow stronger to end your life."

"When you put it like that, I think a little help is in order, don't you?" I asked. "I helped the person who wants to kill me."

"For that I would grant you a boon."

"A boon," I said. "I can accept a boon. What kind of boon?"

"I will tell you where the Demogre is being kept," she said. "That will be the extent of my involvement."

"Really? That's the extent?" I asked, incredulous. "You do realize my mage brother over here can do that?"

Iris smiled in a scarily familiar way, reminding me of Kali.

"I can see why my Mistress chose you, you truly do not fear death," she said. "Yes, Marked One, that is the extent of my assistance. Do you have a quarrel with my choice?"

"That will be more than enough," Monty said, before I could comment on how lame that was as assistance. "Thank you."

"Fine," I said. "No quarrel. Where is it?"

"The Demogre, and the Order who controls it are in the

tunnels beneath this island, where the metal vehicles gather. In the center of the island, there is an open place deep underground. There they have made their home, and it is there they keep the creature."

"Well, that's about as clear as a muddy swamp at night during an eclipse," I said, not holding back. "You can't be any more specific?"

She stared at me for a few seconds, then broke out in laughter.

"I like you, Marked One," she said, clapping me on the shoulder and nearly dislocating it. "I hope you grow strong enough one day to face me in battle, I would truly enjoy that."

"Pass," I said. "Thank you, though. I know you can't get involved so even though it doesn't sound like it, I appreciate the boon."

"I will let my Mistress know what occurred here, but knowing how she is—"

"She already knows?"

She nodded.

"I wish you luck, Marked One," she said and headed down the corridor to Dex's room. "May we meet again soon."

I heard Dex's door close and she was gone.

TWENTY-SIX

"Where exactly are they hiding?" I asked. "Do you know?"

"Hold on, one second," he said raising a finger. "I have a good idea."

He returned from the library with a set of plans, which he unrolled on the counter between his tea cup and my mug of coffee, using both to keep the plans open.

"Judging from her description—" he continued.

"You mean her super accurate, 'go down the road about three miles until you see the gnarled tree, hang a left at the second fork in the road, go down until the road slopes just a bit, right by the small duck pond, there'll be some gopher holes, if you see the red barn you've gone too far' set of directions?"

"Yes. As I was saying..." He paused. "Are you sure you haven't had too much of that javambrosia?"

"No, why do you ask?"

"Aside from your nearly suicidal interaction with an assassin who works for a goddess, you mean?"

"I just didn't appreciate her boon," I said. "Is it too much to ask for a little more detail? We got her sword back. Some boon that was."

"Anyway, theres only one place to hide underground that would accommodate a group like the Sanguinary Order and have enough room to house a Demogre."

"Oh? There's a readymade evil lair under the city?" I asked. "Who knew? Where is this place?"

"Under Grand Central Terminal, there are a pair of substations, respectively known as Substation 1T and 1L," he said, pointing to a location on the plans. "These substations would be a perfect hiding place. They are deep underground, difficult to get to, and almost impossible to detect unless you know what to look for. Honestly, it would have been impossible to locate them without Iris pointing us in the right direction."

"Even with your mage ability?"

"Even with my ability," he confirmed. "If they are down there, a few well-placed runes could hide them from any mage scans. I could pass right over them and not know it."

"How do *you* even know about this place?"

"These substations were closed after the war," he said. "Over the years, they were abandoned and then sealed, left to time. A sorceress like Caligo could get past old seals and help them establish a base of operations down there."

"No one would find them down there," I said. "It could explain why Esti had to lay a trap for us. They could be traveling using the subway, taking the Demogre underground. Would it fit in the subway tunnels?"

"Yes," Monty said, with a nod, tracing a route on the plans. "We would have to go down Grand Central Terminal without being detected. This place is still considered off-limits."

"Is the Dark Goat in the garage?" I asked. "Unless you want to take the subway?"

The sun peeked over the horizon.

"Just in time for rush hour? I'd rather not, thank you."

"You can't consider yourself a true New Yorker until you've ridden the subway at rush hour," I said. "Get the experience of really being among the people."

"You mean get the experience of dealing with irate commuters crushing and rushing in cramped subway cars as they go to work at jobs they detest, and feel the need to share all of the good will with their fellow New Yorkers? That experience?"

"Exactly, nothing like the smell of angry subway in the early morning," I said. "It gets your heart pumping and your fists flexing."

"I decline the subway experience," he said, hanging up the phone. "Andrei says the car is in the garage and that Olga wants to speak with us when we have a moment."

"Do we have a moment?"

"Not really no," he said taking a sip from his cup. "Not that it will stop her from finding us on our way to the car."

"Can't you just teleport us to the location at Grand Central?"

"No, too risky. That many old runes would create a type of runic interference," he said. "We could end up inside a wall or worse."

"Okay let's not do that," I said, with a shudder. "How about this? Can you teleport us inside the Dark Goat?"

"No, for pretty much the same reason," he said. "The runes in and on the vehicle would prevent that type of teleport. Cecil is exceptional at his craft. I'm sure he designed it that way, as some type of failsafe. Could you imagine some enemy mage teleporting into the backseat while we're driving?"

"Only if the mage in question wanted to become lunch for Peaches, who takes up the entire backseat as his kingdom," I said. "But I get it, I can see it as a defensive measure Cecil would think of, for sure."

"Pack your kit and let's go," he said. "Are you keeping the Zegna on?"

"It's growing on me," I said. "I'll keep it on for now. Don't get too used to this though, I'm not a mage."

"I'll keep that in mind."

We made it to the Dark Goat when Olga came around a corner and approached us.

"How does she always know?" I muttered under my breath. "This is all you...good luck."

"Simon...don't you—"

I opened the suicide door and shoved my hellhound into the backseat. His Royal Highness Sprawlington the First, spread out over his entire kingdom of the backseat. I quickly jumped behind the wheel and began to make myself look busy by putzing around under the dashboard, effectively hiding my face and leaving Monty to deal with Olga on his own.

Even though I could still hear them, I made sure I looked uber busy with something technical of importance by pulling out some wires, putting some in my teeth and holding a bunch of extra ones in my hand.

"Hello, Olga," Monty said. "You are looking well."

"Da," she said cutting him off. "How is little Cecelia?"

"She is well, my uncle is taking good care of her and her studies."

"You are her teacher, you must teach," she said and peeked inside the car where I sat. "And Stronk too. You both must teach."

"We will," he said. "We are a little pressed for time, can we discuss this in detail at a later time?"

"Yes," she said. "I will see you when you come back. We

must talk. Cecelia's family wants to visit new school. To check security for little Cecelia."

"They want to make sure little Cecelia is secure?" Monty asked. "Are they certain?"

"Very certain," Olga said. "I told them no worry, Cecelia is safe. They want to see how safe."

"I'm not sure that is a good idea," Monty said, warily. "They should really reconsider."

"They will not, they have heads like stone, very hard, not change mind," she said. "You help convince them, then they will agree."

"Very well," he said as he opened the passenger door. "We can discuss details at another time."

"Good," she said and tapped on my window. "Stronk."

I came up from under the dash trying to look extra flustered and busy.

"Oh, hi, Olga," I said, removing some wire from my mouth. "Was just fixing some wiring down here."

"You are bad liar and worse mechanic," she said, narrowing her eyes and pointing at the wires. "Those wires are *bessmyslennyy*—mean nothing. You keep eye on Cecelia, do not forget you are teacher also."

"I'll make sure to keep an eye on her too," I said. "It's good to see you."

"I keep my eyes on you," she said, and turned to walk away. "I always see you, Stronk."

She reached the stairwell door and went upstairs.

"How did I become Cece's teacher all of sudden?" I said rearranging the wires. Contrary to Olga's opinion, I knew exactly what I was doing, and only messed around with wires that I knew were non-essential. "How did *that* happen?"

"It probably all began when you encouraged her to…what were your words again? Unleash the beast or something to that effect?"

"I was just encouraging her to let the power flow."

"Which she did, right off your dawnward and into the side of the Moscow, resulting in some creative renovation Olga didn't appreciate, if I recall."

"At least she didn't destroy the building," I said. "That would've been an eviction for sure."

"I think eviction would have been the least of our worries if we had destroyed the Moscow," he said. "Are you almost done with your faux wiring repair?"

"I know what I'm doing," I said sitting up. "I was just trying to minimize the chastising."

"You did a splendid job there," he said. "Grand Central Terminal?"

I turned on the engine and let it roar in all its automotive glory. I sat and basked for a few seconds before I nodded and put the car in drive.

We roared out of the garage and headed to face a Demogre.

TWENTY-SEVEN

We parked on Vanderbilt Street just off 42nd Street and entered Grand Central Terminal from one of the side entrances.

A few people stared at my hellhound but true to form most ignored the overly large hellhound, as long as he didn't smile, use his baleful glare, or shatter eardrums with one of his barks.

Monty gestured as we approached the information kiosk in the center of the floor. I noticed a few seconds later that everyone started to slow down.

"Since when could you stop time?" I said looking around at everyone moving in slow motion. "How?"

"I didn't stop time," he said moving his hands quickly on the rear of the kiosk and opening a door. "I sped us up, this is a variation of teleporting in place very rapidly. Inside, now."

We stepped into the small room at the rear of the kiosk and headed over to a spiral staircase that led down. We followed the stairs for some time until I was sure we were way below the tracks of Grand Central.

"Where are we?" I asked. "We are way past the trains' level now."

"Lower level," he said. "The tracks down here were used to transport weaponry and heavy grade military equipment."

"I never knew all this was down here."

"Most don't," he said, taking us down one of the tunnels. "This entire area was clandestine until a few decades ago. It's still off-limits."

"Are we still—?"

He held out an arm to stop us from moving.

"Heretics," he said, pushing us back against the wall. "They haven't sensed us yet. Where is she?"

"Where is who?" I asked. "Who are you looking for?"

I noticed a few things in that moment.

One, I was wearing an obscenely expensive suit and Monty was pushing me back against a grubby and dirty underground subway wall making me unhappy about ruining my suit. Two, either Monty's ability to sense other beings had increased considerably, or mine was getting much worse. Three, we were actually sandwiched between two patrolling groups of Heretics of the Order, and were about to be discovered in about one minute.

"Monty," I said, keeping my voice low and motioning to the side with my head. "There's another—"

"I know," he said, keeping his voice just as low. "When I distract them, we head for that side tunnel over there. She'll be close then."

"Who'll be close? What tunnel?"

He remained silent, pointing across the tracks until I saw the tunnel he meant.

I nodded.

He formed a brilliant white orb of power and flung it into the center of the track. It split in two halfway there and shot in opposite directions, headed at the two groups.

We ran across the tracks and ducked into the darkness of the side tunnel. Behind us the Heretics were yelling and calling for reinforcements. We headed deeper into the tunnels until Monty stopped abruptly.

"No sudden movements," he said. "Keep your hands visible, and your weapons hidden."

"What is it?" I hissed. "How are we going to defend ourselves if we can't use weapons."

"We don't have any weapons that can protect us against this," he said, moving forward. "Just let me do the talking."

This time I sensed the energy signature and it was overwhelming. He was right. Anything we had would be insignificant against the power of the being I was sensing.

It felt strange and powerful, but also familiar, like a warm blanket on a cold day, a refreshing cup of hot coffee during a winter storm. The familiar smell of freshly baked chocolate chip cookies tickled my nose.

Then I knew who was in the dark tunnel and I smiled.

"Hello, Mage," an older voice said. "Ah, you've gone through some difficulty, but you're learning." She chuckled to herself and tapped her cane lightly on the floor. "You're doing it hard, as is your way and nature, but it's happening."

My eyes had become accustomed to the darkness by now, and I could see the huddled woman sitting in the dark. Her eyes gave off a soft golden glow.

Monty nodded his head and crouched down to her level.

"Hello, Grandmother," he said. "You look well."

"I look the same as I always look, you silver-tongued rapscallion," she said, looking around Monty and focusing on me. "The Marked of Kali and his bondmate, come closer child. Let me look at you all."

"Hello, Grandmother," I said. "I didn't bring any chocolate. If I had known—"

"Hush, now," she said tapping my chest with her cane. "I

made no request. Death has touched you, no, he walks with you now. Some hard choices wait for you."

"They've been pretty hard so far."

"They will be harder," she said her voice sad, but then she cheered up. "But you have your family, your brother, your bondmate, and your heart. You are never truly alone, despite what the Destroyer showed you, remember the curse is also a favor."

"How did you—?"

"Shh," she said, and tapped her cane again and waited for a few seconds. "Much better. You mustn't stay here long. Those who dwell with the demon roam these tunnels."

"Grandmother, I do have a request, one I don't know you can fulfill," Monty said. " I need to procure a shift for all of us."

"The pup too?" she asked. "That will cost."

"Yes," he said. "Can you do it?"

"Do you have something for me?"

"Once I cast this tribute, they will know where we are down here," he said. "Especially if the Demogre is patrolling the tunnels with the Heretics."

"Child, they are aware of your presence," she said. "I just sent a group of them somewhere cold and unpleasant. Do you have something for me? If not, I cannot shift any of you."

Monty closed his eyes and pressed his hands together. I felt the shift in power as he gestured, forming three small rectangular boxes. The smell of chocolate filled the tunnel. I looked at the boxes and noticed they each were wrapped with a golden lattice.

The Transporter narrowed her eyes at Monty, stood, and shook her head, placing a hand on his arm.

"This is too much, child," she said. "I will accept your tribute, but you will allow me a gift as well."

"She's going to give you—?"

I immediately stopped talking as she gazed at me with those glowing eyes. She tapped each of us with her cane, whispering some words under her breath.

"Your shifts have been procured," she said. "Your gifts will be present when you need them." She turned to look down the tunnel and tapped her cane again. This time I felt the shift of the Heretics disappearing. "It is time to go. You know how to activate the shift when you need it?"

Monty nodded.

"Good, go do what you are here to do."

"Thank you, Grandmother," Monty said. "Please enjoy the—"

"No, thank you, child...now hurry, more are coming."

She tapped her cane and disappeared along with the three boxes of golden chocolate.

Monty headed down the tunnel and gestured creating a sphere of silence around us. The sphere muffled our footsteps as we moved fast through the tunnel.

We headed down the tunnels in silence for a few minutes before he came to a stop. He looked out into the darkness as if searching for something and then nodded to himself, before we headed forward again.

"A little farther," he said. "Let's regroup here."

"What kind of chocolate did you give her?" I asked. "She gave us a gift? Since when do Transporters give out gifts?"

"It's rare, but it does happen, usually it's in direct relation to the chocolate you offer as payment for the shift you procure."

"What did you offer?"

"Pure Criollo cacao, which is considered the rarest chocolate in the world," he said. "It's also incredibly difficult to materialize. That cast took me months of study and I could only form those small bars."

"So you just gave her the equivalent of a 1904 Rolls Royce 15hp?"

"If that's a rare car, then yes."

"It's one of the rarest," I said. "There's only one left."

"That chocolate isn't quite *that* rare, but it's not usually used as payment for Transporter shifts. Most mages don't bother creating something that exquisite for them. Transporters are judged by their dress and environment, it's a mistake many make."

"Why did you procure shifts?" I asked. "Peaches can shift us out."

"We're going to face a creature that negates magic," he said. "Even the Demogre's ability would fail in the face of a Transporter shift. It never hurts to have some insurance."

"Why didn't she read us this time?"

"She didn't need to," he said. "She knows who we are and who we are becoming it seems."

I nodded thinking about her statement about the curse and the favor. I hadn't told anyone about that part of the conversation with Kali.

"Are you ready?" he asked, shaking out his hands. "Remember, you have to get close before I can neutralize it."

"Like I could forget that fun fact," I said, tightening my holster and making sure Grim Whisper was handy. I let my senses expand and felt Ebonsoul inside. "I'm ready."

"And your creature?"

Peaches let out a low rumble and chuffed.

"He's ready."

"Good," he said. "Let's go stop Esti and the Order."

TWENTY-EIGHT

We moved forward until we faced a bare wall.

"Monty? Did we take a wrong turn?" I asked looking around. "This is a dead end."

"You have no idea how right you are," a voice said behind us. "Open the door and release the creature."

Esti.

Runes flared to life as a section of the wall slid away. Beyond the wall, was an enormous space large enough to fit Cecil's Shrike. The space was outfitted with an armory, bunks, several kitchens, and an oversized training area.

"They look like they're gearing up for a war," I said as I scanned the area and stepped inside. "Where are all the Heretics?"

"They're right here," Esti said stepping into the middle of the room, wearing a large cloak that covered most of her body. "Show yourselves."

One by one the Heretics decloaked, revealing themselves in the lowlight of the hangar space. There were at least a hundred of them. Not as many as the Blood Hunters, but there were only three of us against all of them.

They all held drawn bows pointed in our direction as the door closed behind us. I glanced back to see a seamless wall. We weren't getting out that way.

"This space is runed to prevent casting," Monty said. "Not as powerful as a neutral zone but it will make it difficult."

"We expected a mage to show up eventually," Esti said. "I'm glad we could test out our defenses on you, Montague."

"That's some sophisticated cloaking," I said, turning to face her again. "How did you manage that?"

"Simple," she said. "We merely acquired and applied the runes from none of your damn business."

She threw off her cloak and my stomach did a quick flipflop of fear. One side of her torso was perfectly normal, but her other side, the side missing the arm, was covered in a writhing darkness. She looked down at her darkside and it coalesced into an arm holding a sword.

"Okay," I said, forming Ebonsoul as Monty pulled out his Sorrows and they softly wailed. "I did not expect that."

"I owe this to you, Strong," Esti said, looking down at her dark arm. "After the Blood Hunters turned their backs on me, I found a new family and a new arm. The Order took me in. Their sorceress healed me, made me whole, and gave me a new purpose."

"Donating your time to charity and helping the sick?"

"Before I kill you, I'm going to rip out your tongue and see how funny you sound when you're choking on your own blood."

"Wow, that's pretty dark, even for a deranged ex-Blood Hunter no one wants," I said. "I hope you kept the receipt." I glanced at Monty who nodded back. "That arm, like its owner, looks defective."

"None of you are leaving here alive, I'm even going to gut your dog, Strong, and leave your bodies here to rot and feed the rats."

"Or, hear me out," I said, holding up a hand. "We can go with plan B, where you surrender and hand yourself over to Valentina."

"Valentina?" she scoffed. "Have you lost your mind?"

"For the record, I did try," I said, mostly to Monty. "Can you deflect those arrows?"

"Yes, I acquired the signature from the one that was buried in your arm," he said under his breath. "We have to engage her before the Demogre arrives."

"Good plan," I said and raised my voice. "Okay, Plan C, you want me dead, right? Come kill me yourself, just you and me to the death."

"You *still* don't understand, Strong," she said, walking forward. "You are going to die. They're just here to make it interesting until the Demogre gets here. Kill the mage and the dog."

She ran at me then and I just managed to dodge an arrow aimed at my head.

"Monty? A little shielding would be nice."

"In a moment," he said. "A little busy right now. In the meantime, you could always deploy your dawnward?"

He was right, but Esti wasn't about to give me the opportunity as she crashed into me and tried to bury her dark blade into my chest.

Monty was deflecting several arrows and I saw Peaches blink in and out as he pounced on several of the Heretics, chomping and mangling them, before slamming them into the ground, all without removing parts of their bodies.

Esti stepped close trying to push me back with her blade. She had the advantage of length on her weapon and I had to keep maneuvering around to prevent her from impaling me.

"This is only the opening overture," she said, stepping back and unleashing a vicious spinning side kick which caught me in my midsection and sent me flying back. "I was going to let the Demogre kill you, but you know what? I think I'm going to enjoy killing you myself."

"That's mighty nice of you," I said as I rolled to my feet and paused a moment to drive her over the edge. "Did Caligo tell you she was just using you and the Order? The whole plan was to eliminate me, you are as much a pawn as Dira. You were meant to be used and thrown away. Seems like your new family doesn't care about you either."

She stood absolutely still for a few seconds and I realized I may have gone too far. I saw the madness rear its head in her eyes and I knew in that moment she was gone.

"Fuck you, Strong," she growled. "Die! I want you to DIE!"

She screamed then, and the world went insane. The Demogre exploded through the door, crushing and swatting Heretics across the room. Some of them died when they hit the far walls, and others died from the sudden impact of the blow from the Demogre's fist. The Heretics went from attacking Monty, me and Peaches, to including the Demogre in their list of targets.

Esti ignored all of that and came at me, attempting to make good on her last promise that I should die. I felt the power of the Demogre in the space around me, draining the very energy from the air.

I stumbled back as Esti approached and laughed.

"You're feeling it, aren't you, Marked of Kali?" she mocked. "The Demogre nullifies magic, I'm going to enjoy killing you."

She closed in and thrust forward aiming at my neck. I barely parried her dark arm blade. I stepped back and scanned the floor. The Demogre was wreaking havoc with the Heretics. Monty was struggling as the null-field affected him and I couldn't see where Peaches was. It took half-a-second, then I saw him blink in and out again just as fast.

I was getting tired and my blade arm was heavy.

"I will kill everyone and everything in your life," Esti said as she repeatedly struck down on Ebonsoul. "I will rip everything from your life the same way you tore everything from mine."

"You tried to kill Chi," I said. "Why? Because she's different? What kind of sick reason is that?"

"She's different?" Esti yelled. "How deluded are you? She's not just different, she's a vampire! She deserves to die and you deserve to die with her!"

She rushed forward and dropped her guard, allowing me to plunge Ebonsoul right into her midsection.

"What have you done?" I asked shocked. "You don't know—"

"Oh, I know," she said, driving her dark arm into my side. "I told you, Strong, you were dying today. I never said anything about me surviving."

"You crazy bitch," I said, trying to push her away as she laughed and clamped her arms around me. "To me, Demon! To me!"

The Demogre roared from across the room and slapped some Heretics away as it turned at the sound of her voice.

"Today," she said, as her laughter raced into hysteria. "Today, the Marked of Kali dies! Today, I kill the only person Michiko Nakatomi loved. You will die with her name on your lips, Strong, and I will see your life escape your eyes. Die!"

<I need you here, boy. Push the monster back for me just a little bit.>

I didn't know if he had heard me, but I wasn't going to wait and find out as the Demogre closed in to swipe my head from my shoulders.

"Not today, Esti," I said and pulled her arm out of my side with a grunt and nearly collapsed. There was no warmth and it felt as if my curse had shut off. "I'm not dying today."

I managed a weak shove and pushed her away from me.

So much blood was pouring out of my side. Esti stumbled back, still laughing as I felt the Demogre close in on me. She fell to her knees as Ebonsoul nearly disemboweled her. It didn't act as a siphon because the Demogre had shut the place down.

"Goodbye, Strong," she said, holding her midsection with one arm. The darkness writhed all around her as she lost control of it. "This may be my last day, but I'm making sure you join me."

Surrender to me and I can save you. All I need is some blood.

Shut the hell up. You're not getting blood from me now or ever.

Ebonsoul went quiet and the world shattered with an ear-splitting bark. Peaches materialized behind me and barreled headfirst into the Demogre which was a few feet away from introducing me to the business end of its fists.

It staggered back as I drew on the last of my strength.

I rotated and did the last thing the Demogre expected—I jumped at it. I plunged Ebonsoul into its chest and felt the surge of power rush into my body.

"Monty!" I screamed. "Do it!"

It roared in surprise and pain, and then proceeded to backhand me off its chest, and send me flying across the room.

Esti screamed in delight.

"Yes! Die, Strong!"

I landed hard on the floor and bounced several times before Peaches caught up to me. I saw the light explode from where I lay and saw Monty cast an enormous golden orb of power.

"No!" Esti screamed. This time she wasn't nearly as happy as when I took flight. "You bastard!"

The Demogre fell to its knees, its arms hanging by its side.

Monty leaned forward and whispered something to it. The Demogre shook its enormous head and stared into Monty's face. Monty produced the Sorrows and placed each blade to either side of the Demogre's neck.

The Demogre nodded and Monty removed its head with one move.

"No!" Esti screamed again, this time she was crying. "No, he was supposed to kill Strong and that bitch Nakatomi."

After seeing the Demogre lose its head, the rest of the Heretics lost all desire for battle and fled for the exits, leaving Esti alone.

I slowly got to my feet as my body flushed with heat.

TWENTY-NINE

I limped over to where Esti lay.

My side was still tender, but I wasn't ventilated and leaking blood.

She laughed when she saw me and coughed up some more blood in the process. Her body was a mangled mess and the darkness that covered her torso had crept down to cover part of her leg too.

"Damn it," she said. "You are a hard bastard to kill."

"I've heard that before," I said. "That darkness—"

"I need you to do me a favor, Strong, " she rasped. "This darkness is devouring me, part of the price I had to pay."

"Steep," I said, looking at the darkness. It was slowly advancing down her leg. "Pain?"

"Excruciating," she said. "If I could do it myself I would end it now." She chuckled, and held up one hand. "I appear to be a bit short-handed. I don't want to die in agony, Strong. Make this quick."

I drew Ebonsoul.

"One more thing before I go, Strong," she said, before spitting up more blood. "They're after you. Caligo is only the tip of that hellish iceberg. You need to level up, and you need to do it before it's too late."

"I will," I said, with a nod. "Ready?"

"Don't screw this up, Strong."

"I won't."

"Do it, make it—"

I removed her head in one strike.

Peaches padded over to where I swayed and helped me stay upright. I patted him on the head and gave him a silent thanks.

Monty, with the nulling effect of the Demogre gone, began gesturing.

"What are you doing?" I asked. "I thought you said we can teleport out of here?"

"This isn't a teleport for us," he said. "This is for them."

"For them?"

"I'm sending her remains to Valentina and the Demogre to Salius," he said, as he focused on the gestures. "Both will be laid to rest with the dignity they deserve."

I nodded.

It was the right thing to do.

A few moments later, both bodies were gone.

"What about all these Heretics?" I said, scanning the room and the bodies that lay everywhere. "What are we going to do with them?"

"We? Nothing," he said. "The surviving Heretics will return to claim their dead once we leave."

"Does this mean the Order is finished?" I asked. "We wiped them out?"

"Unlikely," he said. "I'm sure there are more out there. What we have done is neutralized this cell and sent Caligo a message."

"What message?" I asked. "Try harder next time?"

"No," he said. "The Marked of Kali is not an easy target...*and* try harder next time."

A smile crossed his lips as he stopped me from swaying to the side.

"I'm not going to make it all the way to street level. Can you teleport us from here?"

"We just need to get out of this room and we can use the Transporter's shift to get home," he said. "Can you make it to the door?"

"*That*, I can do."

"Good. Let's go home."

THIRTY

THREE DAYS LATER

I sat on a bench at the campus of the Montague School of Battle Magic. My ferocious hellhound was off being chased around the grounds by the Mayhem Twins, as I had gotten used to calling Cece and Peanut.

Monty was in one of the labs with Dex, devising some variation of a teleport cast. When he tried to explain it to me in an effort to convince me to go with him, my brain began leaking out of my ears. I told him thanks, but no thanks.

I thought about visiting Salius, but the Menagerie had been closed off until his latest creations became accustomed to the boundaries he had established. Something about teaching them the extent of their territory and helping them imprint. It sounded about as complicated as the teleportation variant.

Another pass.

The Morrigan was thankfully busy preparing curricula for the school, and from what I understood, designing the entrance exams for prospective students.

I shuddered at the thought, feeling sorry for the new students who had to go through the exams with the Morrigan and Dex, I assumed, as their proctors.

I did not envy the prospective students at all.

I opted for a quiet stroll through the grounds and settled on one of the stone benches near the Morrigan's Grove. I didn't sit in it because I knew she was a bit touchy about her grove, but I sat just outside and admired it from a distance.

I closed my eyes and enjoyed the silence.

This was the first time in a long time, I wasn't running or fighting for my life. I wasn't facing enemies bent on taking me out and for a brief few seconds, there was actual peace.

I knew it was too good to last.

"I can certainly see the attraction," a voice said next to me on the bench. "I'll have to speak to Dexter to see if he doesn't mind me visiting regularly."

Durga.

"Regularly?" I asked. "You have that amazing temple in Jersey, why make the trips all the way out here? Wherever out here is."

"If I didn't know any better, I'd say you didn't want me to visit," she said. "Is that the case?"

"Honestly? I'd prefer you didn't or at the very least, give me a heads up before you do?"

"You're demanding I tell you when I'm coming to visit?"

"No, not demanding, requesting," I said. "As a courtesy."

She nodded and we sat in silence admiring the grove.

"How did it feel to be mortal? If only briefly?"

"Not fun," I said, after a few moments of thought. "Esti stabbed me in the side, and the Demogre nearly backhanded me across the continent. It hurt."

"Pain gives life meaning, or so I hear."

"Is Rakta really that dangerous?"

"For me, or for you?"

"For me."

"For you, he is fatal," she said. "For me, he is a nuisance. I see you retrieved Iris's sword from Dira."

"You asked me to."

"I've asked you to do many things," she said. "Compliance is not one of your strong suits." She paused as if considering her next question. "Why didn't you kill Dira? You had the opportunity."

"Didn't feel right," I said, giving it some more thought. "She wasn't in her right mind and her body was weak. Killing her in that state felt wrong."

"Good," she said, with a nod and glanced at me. "The Marked of Kali will be held to a higher standard. Always."

"That's good to know," I said. "I've been thinking about something the Transporter said."

"The curse is also a favor?"

"You presented it as a dichotomy."

"Did I?"

"I'm pretty sure you did."

"And what do you think of her words?"

"You may have cursed me alive," I said. "I understand how it can be a curse, but I think the deeper part of being an immortal is what I do with the time I have, however long that is. In that case, it's definitely a favor."

She sat silently next to me and closed her eyes.

"Close your eyes."

I did as instructed.

"Do you hear that?" she asked. "Listen."

I focused, but didn't hear anything out of the ordinary.

"No, what am I listening to?"

"That is the sound of the Marked of Kali gaining wisdom."

I opened my eyes but she was gone.

I heard distant laughter and shook my head. I spent the rest of the afternoon enjoying my time on the bench in front of the Morrigan's Grove, knowing moments like this were few and far between.

THE END

AUTHOR NOTES

Thank you for reading this story and jumping into the world of Monty & Strong with me.

Disclaimer: The Author Notes are written at the very end of the writing process. This section is not seen by the ART or my amazing Jeditor. Any typos or errors following this disclaimer are mine and mine alone.

How does it feel when everyone turns against you, and the only people you can turn to are the outcasts? <checks notes> Whoops! That's the next book OUTCAST...sorry!

<sorts notes>

Let's discuss IMMORTAL.

What does it mean to live forever? Cue in Freddie Mercury in the background. I so wanted to include every Highlander reference I could, I really did, but it didn't serve the story (I did manage to get one in, I mean really), but I had to nix most of them.

I will find a way to include them in next story that touches on immortality heavily titled-MORTAL (but that won't be a LONG time).

In **this** story, Simon is realizing that there is a much bigger world out there.

And it wants him dead.

Before I dive in...first—THANK YOU!

This is book 23.

I'm going to let that sink in for a moment...this is book 23. WOW!

Okay, I wanted to express my humblest thanks to you my amazing reader for going on this adventure of 23 books in this series so far and counting! I never imagined we would get this far, but I'm so glad you decided to join me as we do this insanity!

Let's get back to IMMORTAL.

Simon has to realize what it means to be immortal, even more pressing is the fact that there are some major players entering the fringes of his world and he is just now realizing that there are schemes, plans, and machinations afoot, all with one purpose—to destroy the Marked of Kali.

And it's not even his fault...mostly.

I really enjoyed this book because it wasn't as magic heavy(even though I really enjoy the magic) and more looking into Simon and his understanding of the balance between what is a curse and a favor.

I do apologize for those scenes (Monty & Chi), but they had to be done. You did notice Simon was not going to watch the scene with Peaches...me either. The first two were rough enough, if I did the Peaches scene, I don't think I could finish it. Even the little that I showed, was a gut check.

Hard pass.

Simon is growing, Peaches too. Monty will have some harsh lessons in the next story as the Terrible Trio are outcast. This is a major event and will have serious ripple effects for them. Everyone turns their back on them, well not everyone, but most.

They become persona non grata and have to uncover how this happened, why it happened, and who is behind the exiling. It's not just Monty, Simon has a part to play in this, as does Peaches. I'm looking forward to uncovering more of their enemies and why this happens.

Also the Mayhem Twins will have an important part to play in the story, especially Pnut, who totally understands what it means to be an outcast and unwanted.

There will be a serious threat from the Council of Sects who are…no sorry that would give too much away. The next book will be out soon™.

Let's just say it's a major threat and will require some serious firepower to deal with them—firepower Monty & Simon don't have, but will need. For that to happen, Monty has to tap into dormant power and Simon needs to unlock aspects of the battleform that haven't been accessible..until now.

There will be a serious conversation with a certain god of the underworld and part of his agenda will be revealed, as well as a certain Chooser of the Slain recruiting a particular immortal to take on a mission—whether he wants to or not.

Now, what is being worked on?

There are a few projects simmering: OUTCAST M&S 24 of course, is in the outline phase, STONE (the second John Kane book) is also being worked on, the secret romantasy book (REDACTED) which I haven't completely revealed (and won't for a little while longer) is about 10% done—plenty of world building for that one.

Some awesome Patreon stories are being prepped for the year (three more stories left for the year!)

In addition, I'm going to try and squeeze in a Night Warden story before Frank flambés me, that story, DIVINE HELL promises to be dark and exciting, exploring how Koda is growing and who wants all of the Night Wardens(all two of them?) retired...permanently.

Somewhere in the wide expanse of my imagination, the Black Jacks are glaring me with arms crossed and standing next to them is Gideon Shepherd and his crew are brandishing weapons and giving me dirty looks.

I haven't forgotten them among so many other stories so my next projects (I CANNOT in good faith make this promise wholeheartedly, but I'm going to make the effort) I will refrain from starting new series until all the started ones are trilogies and closed. There are quite a few of those so I will focus on those for the rest of this year and probably at least the first half of the next. Since most of these are novellas they will be written alongside the full length novels.

As always, I couldn't do this incredibly insane adventure without you, my amazing reader. You jump into these adventures with me, when I say "WHAT IF?" you say: "Hmmm what if indeed. Let's find out where that idea goes!"

For that, I humbly and deeply thank you.

As always, I consider myself deeply fortunate to have the most amazing readers that are willing to leap into these worlds with the same reckless abandon I have in writing them. You truly spoil me. Few writers I know have such incredible readers that make it possible to explore and try creating new worlds, and introduce different characters.

Thank you so much for joining me as we load up the extra thermos (better bring three or four of them—industrial-sized) filled with the delicious inky Death Wish Javambrosia, some of you can call shotgun, but a few of you are going to have to shove the enormous hellhound in the back of the Dark Goat over if you want a seat (bring sausage/pastrami-for a guaranteed seat!), as we strap in to jump into all sorts of adventures!

We have plans to thwart, people to rescue, and property to renovate!

In the immortal sage words of our resident Zen Hellhound Master...

Meat is Life!

Thank you again for jumping into this story with me!

SUPPORT US

Patreon
The Magick Squad

Website/Newsletter
www.orlandoasanchez.com

JOIN US

Facebook
Montague & Strong Case Files

Youtube
Bitten Peaches Publishing Storyteller

Instagram
bittenpeaches

Email
orlando@orlandoasanchez.com

M&S World Store
Emandes

BITTEN PEACHES PUBLISHING

Thanks for Reading!

If you enjoyed this book, would you please **leave a review** at the site you purchased it from? It doesn't have to be long… just a line or two would be fantastic and it would really help me out.

Bitten Peaches Publishing offers more books and audiobooks

across various genres including: urban fantasy, science fiction, adventure, & mystery!

www.BittenPeachesPublishing.com

More books by Orlando A. Sanchez

Montague & Strong Detective Agency Novels

Tombyards & Butterflies•Full Moon Howl•Blood is Thicker•Silver Clouds Dirty Sky•Homecoming•Dragons & Demigods•Bullets & Blades•Hell Hath No Fury•Reaping

Wind•The Golem•Dark Glass•Walking the Razor•Requiem•Divine Intervention•Storm Blood•Revenant•Blood Lessons•Broken Magic•Lost Runes•Archmage•Entropy•Corpse Road•Immortal

Montague & Strong Detective Agency Stories
No God is Safe•The Date•The War Mage•A Proper Hellhound•The Perfect Cup•Saving Mr. K

Night Warden Novels
Wander•ShadowStrut•Nocturne Melody

Rule of the Council
Blood Ascension•Blood Betrayal•Blood Rule

The Warriors of the Way
The Karashihan•The Spiritual Warriors•The Ascendants•The Fallen Warrior•The Warrior Ascendant•The Master Warrior

John Kane
The Deepest Cut•Blur

Sepia Blue
The Last Dance•Rise of the Night•Sisters•Nightmare•Nameless•Demon

Chronicles of the Modern Mystics
The Dark Flame•A Dream of Ashes

The Treadwell Supernatural Directive

The Stray Dogs•Shadow Queen•Endgame Tango

Brew & Chew Adventures
Hellhound Blues

Bangers & Mash
Bangers & Mash

Tales of the Gatekeepers
Bullet Ballet•The Way of Bug•Blood Bond

Division 13
The Operative•The Magekiller

Blackjack Chronicles
The Dread Warlock

The Assassin's Apprentice
The Birth of Death

Gideon Shepherd Thrillers
Sheepdog

DAMNED
Aftermath

Nyxia White
They Bite•They Rend•They Kill

Iker the Cleaner
Iker the Unseen•Daystrider•Nightwalker

Fate of the Darkmages
Fated Fury

Stay up to date with new releases!
Shop www.orlandoasanchez.com for more books and audiobooks!

ART SHREDDERS

I want to take a moment to extend a special thanks to the ART SHREDDERS.

No book is the work of one person. I am fortunate enough to have an amazing team of advance readers and shredders.

Thank you for giving of your time and keen eyes to provide notes, insights, answers to the questions, and corrections (dealing wonderfully with my extreme dreaded comma allergy). You help make every book and story go from good to great. Each and every one of you helped make this book fantastic, and I couldn't do this without each of you.

THANK YOU

ART SHREDDERS

Amber, Anne Morando, Audrey Cienki
    Bethany Showell, Beverly Collie
    Cam Skaggs, Cat, Chris Christman II
    Daniel Parr, Denise King, Donna Young Hatridge

Hal Bass, Helen

James Wheat, Jasmine Breeden, Jasmine Davis, Jeanette Auer, Jen Cooper, Joy Kiili, Julie Peckett

Karen Hollyhead

Larry Diaz Tushman, Laura Tallman I

Malcolm Robertson, Mari de Valerio, Maryelaine Eckerle-Foster, Melissa Miller, Melody DeLoach, Michelle Blue

Paige Guido

RC Battels, Rene Corrie, Rob Farnham, Rohan Gandhy

Sondra Massey, Stacey Stein, Susie Johnson

Tami Cowles, Ted Camer, Terri Adkisson

Vikki Brannagan

Wendy Schindler

PATREON SUPPORTERS

Exclusive short stories
Premium Access to works in progress
Free Ebooks for select tiers

Join here
The Magick Squad

THANK YOU

Alisha Harper, Amber Dawn Sessler, Angela Tapping, Anne Morando, Anthony Hudson, Ashley Britt

Brenda French

Carolyn J. Evans, Carrie O'Leary, Christopher Scoggins, Cindy Deporter, Connie Cleary, Cooper Walls, Craig Gill

Dan Bergemann, Dan Fong, Davis Johnson, Diane Garcia, Diane Jackson, Diane Kassmann, Dorothy Phillips

Elizabeth Varga, Enid Rodriguez, Eric Maldonado, Eve Bartlet, Ewan Mollison

Federica De Dominicis, Fluff Chick Productions,

Gail Ketcham Hermann, Gary McVicar, Groove72

Heidi Wolfe

Ingrid Schijven

James Burns, James Wheat, Jasmine Breeden, Jasmine Davis, Jeffrey Juchau, Jo Dungey, Joe Durham, John Fauver(*in memoriam*), Joy Kiili, Just Jeanette

Kathy Ringo, Krista Fox

Leona Jackson, Lisa Simpson, Lizzette Piltch

Malcolm Robertson, Mark Morgan, Mark Price, Mary Beth Wright, MaryAnn Sims, Maureen McCallan, Mel Brown, Melissa Miller, Meri, Duncanson

Paige Guido, Patricia Pearson, Peter Griffin, Pete Peters

Ralph Kroll, Renee Penn, Rick Clapp, Robert Walters

Sara M Branson, Sara N Morgan, Sarah Sofianos, Sassy Bear, Sharon Elliott, Shelby, Sonyia Roy, Stacey Stein, Steven Huber, Susan Bowin, Susan Spry

Tami Cowles, Terri Adkisson, Tommy, Trish Brown

Van Nebedum

W S Dawkins, Wendy Schindler, Wicketbird

***

I want to extend a special note of gratitude to all of our
Patrons in
The Magick Squad.

Your generous support helps me to continue on this amazing adventure called 'being an author'.
I deeply and truly appreciate each of you for your selfless act of patronage.

You are all amazing beyond belief.

THANK YOU

ACKNOWLEDGMENTS

With each book, I realize that every time I learn something about this craft, it highlights so many things I still have to learn. Each book, each creative expression, has a large group of people behind it.

This book is no different.

Even though you see one name on the cover, it is with the knowledge that I am standing on the shoulders of the literary giants that informed my youth, and am supported by my generous readers who give of their time to jump into the adventures of my overactive imagination.

I would like to take a moment to express my most sincere thanks:

To Dolly: My wife and greatest support. You make all this possible each and every day. You keep me grounded when I get lost in the forest of ideas. Thank you for asking the right questions when needed, and listening intently when I go off on tangents. Thank you for who you are and the space you create—I love you.

To my Tribe: You are the reason I have stories to tell. You cannot possibly fathom how much and how deeply I love you all.

To Lee: Because you were the first audience I ever had. I love you, sis.

To the Logsdon Family: The words *thank you* are insufficient to describe the gratitude in my heart for each of you. JL, your support always demands I bring my best, my A-game, and produce the best story I can. Both you and Lorelei (my Uber Jeditor) and now, Audrey, are the reason I am where I am today. My thank you for the notes, challenges, corrections, advice, and laughter. Your patience is truly infinite. *Arigatogozaimasu.*

To Leslie: Thank you for the amazing notes. Your first time in the M&S World was fantastic! Thank you for the insights!

To The Montague & Strong Case Files Group—AKA The MoB (Mages of Badassery): When I wrote T&B there were fifty-five members in The MoB. As of this release, there are over one thousand five hundred members in the MoB. I am honored to be able to call you my MoB Family. Thank you for being part of this group and M&S.

You make this possible. **THANK YOU.**

To the ever-vigilant PACK: You help make the MoB...the MoB. Keeping it a safe place for us to share and just...be.

Thank you for your selfless vigilance. You truly are the Sentries of Sanity.

Chris Christman II: A real-life technomancer who makes the **MoBTV LIVEvents +Kaffeeklatsch** on YouTube amazing. Thank you for your tireless work and wisdom. Everything is connected…you totally rock!

To the WTA—The Incorrigibles: JL, Ben Z., Eric QK., S.S., and Noah.

They sound like a bunch of badass misfits, because they are. My exposure to the deranged and deviant brain trust you all represent helped me be the author I am today. I have officially gone to the *dark side* thanks to all of you. I humbly give you my thanks, and…it's all your fault.

To my fellow Indie Authors: I want to thank each of you for creating a space where authors can feel listened to, and encouraged to continue on this path. A rising tide lifts all the ships indeed.

To The English Advisory: Aaron, Penny, Carrie, Davina, and all of the UK MoB. For all things English…thank you.

To DEATH WISH COFFEE: This book (and every book I write) has been fueled by generous amounts of the only coffee on the planet (and in space) strong enough to power my very twisted imagination. Is there any other coffee that can compare? I think not. DEATH WISH—thank you!

To Deranged Doctor Design: Kim, Darja, Tanja, Jovana, and Milo (Designer Extraordinaire).

If you've seen the covers of my books and been amazed, you can thank the very talented and gifted creative team at

DDD. They take the rough ideas I give them, and produce incredible covers that continue to surprise and amaze me. Each time, I find myself striving to write a story worthy of the covers they produce. DDD, you embody professionalism and creativity. Thank you for the great service and spectacular covers. **YOU GUYS RULE!**

To you, the reader: I was always taught to save the best for last. I write these stories for **you**. Thank you for jumping down the rabbit holes of *what if?* with me. You are the reason I write the stories I do.

You keep reading...I'll keep writing.

Thank you for your support and encouragement.

SPECIAL MENTIONS

To Dolly: my rock, anchor, and inspiration. Thank you...always.

Larry & Tammy—The WOUF: Because even when you aren't there...you're there.

Orlando A. Sanchez
www.orlandoasanchez.com

Orlando has been writing ever since his teens when he was immersed in creating scenarios for playing Dungeons and Dragons with his friends every weekend.

The worlds of his books are urban settings with a twist of the paranormal lurking just behind the scenes and with generous doses of magic, martial arts, and mayhem.

He currently resides in Queens, NY with his wife and children.

Thanks for Reading!

If you enjoyed this book
Please leave a review & share!
(with everyone you know)

It would really help us out!

Printed in Great Britain
by Amazon